1

Author of "The Memory of Roses"

BLAIR MCDOWELL

DELIGHTING IN YOUR COMPANY

rebel ink press

Publisher's Note:
This is a work of fiction. All characters, places, businesses, and incidents are from the author's imagination. Any resemblance to actual places, people, or events is purely coincidental. Any trademarks mentioned herein are not authorized by the trademark owners and do not in any way mean the work is sponsored by or associated with the trademark owners. Any trademarks used are specifically in a descriptive capacity.

ISBN: 9781937265625

First Edition

10 9 8 7 6 5 4 3 2 1

Cover Artist: Carl J. Franklin
Delighting In Your Company © 2012, Blair McDowell
Rebel Ink Press , LLC
Printed in The United States of America

www.rebelinkpress.com

DEDICATION

To the people of Statia, whose stories and legends inspired this book.

Alas, my love, you do me wrong,

To cast me off discourteously,

While I have loved you well and long,

Delighting in your company.

From the song Greensleeves,

attributed to Henry VIII

CHAPTER 1

Pallid light came through windows that were now stark and streaked with dirt as Amalie walked through the house. The walls were bare, the wallpaper faded, its old fashioned pattern bright only where familiar pictures had once hung. She shook her head. It was depressing to see this house where once laughter and love had reigned, now so empty.

What did she expect? The house had been a major bone of contention in the divorce. Brett had brought nothing to the marriage, but thanks to California community property laws the court had awarded him half of everything, including the house she had inherited from her mother. More fool she for having added his name to the title when they were married.

She'd tried, Lord how she had tried, to get a mortgage to buy out Brett's half, but houses in the Hollywood Hills, even small houses like hers, were priced in the millions now. Amalie's income from the ad agency didn't begin to qualify her for the size mortgage she needed to keep the house so she'd been forced to put it on the market. And her lawyer, to put it as kindly as possible, was incompetent when faced with the shark her husband had hired.

The house was empty now except for some things in what used to be her mother's sewing room. Amalie had already moved the few pieces of furniture she wanted to keep to her small rented condo. Her ex-husband had taken all the rest. Indeed, Brett had taken and taken and taken, she thought as she climbed the stairs and walked down the hallway, her footsteps echoing in the silence. It was what he did best. How could she have been so naive?

She paused in the doorway of the small room at the back of the house. It had been her mother's favorite room. Amalie could still see her there, busy at her old Pfaff sewing machine, making curtains for the kitchen, designing slip covers, or putting the finishing touches on a dress. Her mother loved to sew. And Amalie had loved to sit in the rocking chair beside the small dormer window and watch her. They always talked as her mother worked. She'd felt she could talk to her mother about anything.

But that was long ago and she must now get on with going through these remaining shelves and storage boxes, deciding what to keep and what to dispose of. A job she hadn't been able to face when her mother died five years ago.

Pulling a moving box toward the wall of built-in shelving, Amalie began to sort through fabrics, silks and cottons and wools. Some neatly folded, others in bolts, all in the jewel tones her mother had so loved. She smoothed her hand over particularly beautiful red damask. What had her mother intended for this piece? Perhaps a cover for a footstool? Her father had always teased her mother that sewing was simply an excuse for collecting fabrics. Amalie smiled as she thought about her father, always laughing, bigger than life. He had died a year before her mother and her mother had never recovered from his death. She seemed to just fade away after he was gone

That's what Amalie had expected from marriage, a lifetime of devotion. How could she have gotten it so wrong?

Amalie brought her mind back to the task at hand. She started placing the fabrics into one of the larger boxes to take to the local Goodwill shop. They'd make good use of them.

An hour later she'd emptied the shelves of everything but one small cardboard box that seemed to contain old correspondence. As Amalie rifled through the envelopes she saw most were letters of condolence on her father's death. Clearly her mother had been unable to dispose of them. She was about to put the box in a pile of trash for burning when one that hadn't been opened caught her eye. The return address, in spidery handwriting, read "*J. Ansett, St. Clement's, Windward Islands, Caribbean.*

She studied the envelope with curiosity. Ansett? Her family name? As far as she knew they had no relatives in the Caribbean. Who could have been writing to her mother from St. Clement's? She'd never even heard of St. Clement's.

Carefully, Amalie opened the envelope and pulled out the thin tissue-like blue airmail paper.

My dear Mrs. Ansett,

Please allow me to introduce myself. I am Josephina Ansett.

I have reason to believe that we may be related. The Ansetts originally settled on St. Clement's Island in the late seventeen hundreds. My genealogical research has led me to discover that while one Ansett brother, Lord Amery Ansett, remained in England, inheriting the family title and lands, his two younger brothers came to the New World seeking their fortunes. One, James, came to the Caribbean while the other, Edmond, settled in New England. I believe that you married an Ansett who was a descendant of that New England branch of the family, and that therefore your daughter, Amalie, may be a distant cousin of mine.

There are few Ansetts left. I am the last on St. Clement's. I am now approaching my eightieth birthday and should like very much to meet my remaining Ansett cousins.

Please consider coming to the St. Clement's for the week of February twentieth as my guest. Call the number below and I shall be happy to make the necessary travel arrangements for both you and your daughter. I look forward to meeting you.

Yours truly,

Josephina Ansett

Ansett Beach House, St. Clement's
889-540-8265

Amalie stared at the letter in disbelief. She had a cousin in the Caribbean? Her mother never even mentioned the possibility to her. But then her mother may not have known. She'd never opened the envelope.

But who was to say the letter was even genuine? There were all sorts of scams involving so-called lost relatives. Still…

Absently Amalie stuck the envelope in the pocket of her jeans and stood to survey the room. The last traces of her mother, of her own childhood, had been removed. It was time to go.

Outside, she looked at the old Spanish style house that had been her home for twenty-seven years. Then she looked at the unkempt lawn and the *For Sale* sign with the slash of red *Sold* superimposed. It was over. This part of her life was truly over.

She climbed into her battered little Mini and pulled away from the curb.

****

The phone was ringing as Amalie unlocked the door to her condo. She threw down her things and rushed to pick it up just as the answering machine was kicking in. "I'm here, Lorna."

"I was hoping you would be. I'm coming over and thought I might bring Chinese. You have anything in the house to drink?"

13

"Nothing, I'm afraid the cupboard is bare. I was going to go grab Kentucky Fried. But Chinese sounds infinitely better. Can you give me an hour? I need time to shower and change."

"Fine. See you then."

Amalie placed the phone back on the kitchen counter and headed toward the bedroom. How like Lorna to know she needed company on this of all nights, when the final door on her marriage, on her former life, was irrevocably closed.

As she showered and dressed, she thought back to her first meeting with Lorna. They'd been in their second year in the Business and Marketing program at UCLA, two women in a class with twelve men. They joined forces in the interest of self-preservation and stayed friends ever since because they found they thought alike and enjoyed one another's company.

After graduation, with their freshly minted business degrees, both found jobs in Los Angeles advertising agencies. They watched and commiserated with each other as less competent men were promoted over them while they remained underpaid and undervalued. It was Lorna who suggested they should open their own agency.

Ansett-Cummings, Inc. had been in business for five years now and had a respectable client list. Working together on a daily basis had cemented an already close friendship. They encountered few of the problems that so often plague friends who go into business

14

together. Their disagreements were rare and were always settled equitably.

On a personal level, Amalie didn't know how she could have survived the last two years, the separation and bitter divorce, without Lorna's support.

Amalie was pulling on a comfortable oversized sweater when the buzzer rang and Lorna's voice came over the speaker. "Open up, Amalie. I've got my hands full of bags and boxes and bottles"

An hour later they were settled on the sofa with an array of empty and half empty cartons in front of them, glasses of Rose d'Anjou in their hands.

Lorna sat back and surveyed the apartment, not for the first time. "Why do you continue to stay here? It has to be the most depressing place I've ever seen. All this fake leather and chrome and glass."

"It's a furnished rental. That's what they put in furnished rentals."

"But it's been two years. Why are you still in a furnished rental? Surely you have enough money from the settlement to rent or buy something better than this. And why didn't you at least take half of your furniture? You were entitled to that."

Amalie sighed. "I didn't want the furniture. I didn't want anything that reminded me of Brett, of the mess I've made of my life." A tear slid unguarded down her cheek.

"Oh, God. I'm sorry, Amalie. Why are you letting that bastard get to you this way? Surely you can't still love him?"

Amalie gave a small, bitter laugh. "No. He killed any feelings I had for him long ago. It isn't him, it's me. I just don't trust my own judgment anymore. I keep wishing I'd listened to you when you warned me about marrying a second rate actor with a history of using women. When you suggested a pre-nup."

"I must admit it did occur to me that he was probably more interested in acquiring your connections and your house in the Hollywood Hills than he was in acquiring your person. That had nothing to do with you. It had everything to do with him. You weren't the first woman he used to get a leg up. He thought you knew people because of your father's place in the film industry. You know that."

"I guess he didn't understand how completely my father kept his family life separated from his professional life. Any connections I might have had were gone when Dad died. I didn't know anyone who could help Brett's career."

"I never understood why you were so determined to marry him."

"Are you kidding? Didn't you ever take a good look at him? He was the most gorgeous man I'd ever seen. I was amazed that he wanted mousy quiet me."

"Quiet, yes. Mousy? Don't be ridiculous. With all that curly ash blond hair and those big doe-like brown eyes? And all those curves? Don't you know you're beautiful?"

"I'm at least ten pounds overweight and I only come up to your chin."

"You've lived too long in Hollywood. Anyplace but here your weight would be normal. And five-seven is not short. Don't compare yourself to me. At six-one, I'm an Amazon. You want problems finding men? Try being my height."

"Do you suppose all women are unhappy with the way they look?"

"I'm not unhappy with the way I look and you shouldn't be either. I think we're both very attractive, just not in a Hollywood sort of way. It's hard to compete with all that pulchritude."

Amalie laughed in spite of herself. "So you think if I just go someplace else I'll magically be beautiful?"

"I think going away for a while is a good idea on many levels. You need a vacation. You should get away from here for a while. Get some perspective. Maybe find a new man. Don't, for God's sake, get serious though. Just have an affair."

"Men are the last thing on my mind," Amalie replied, shaking her head. Trust Lorna to try to help her put her life in order.

Later that night as she undressed for bed, Amalie looked at the blue envelope on her dresser. She pulled the letter out and read it again.

Where was St. Clement's? It was in the Caribbean, but where? She opened her laptop and did a search on Google Earth. It was about two-thirds of the way down the chain of islands between the Bahamas and the South American coast. It was so tiny that she almost missed it.

Maybe she should try to contact her Ansett cousin. What was her name? Josephina? What an old fashioned name. Of course she'd been eighty when she wrote that letter. She might well no longer be alive. Still…

The next morning at eight-thirty, Amalie was working in the office when Lorna strolled in.

"I brought chocolate croissants and cappuccinos. I'll bet you didn't have any breakfast," Lorna said as she placed the pastries and coffee cups on the desk.

"Guilty as charged. Thanks."

"Ronald Ainsworth is due at ten. He wants to review the campaign we've prepared for their magazine ads and television spots. Are we ready for him?"

"The cat food ads. Sure. It's all here. Everything we discussed with him, providing he doesn't change his mind again. We can run it by him this morning in our screening room."

"Good. I know he's a bit of a pain, but he's one of our best clients, and he always pays his bills on time, which is more than I can say for some of them."

"He can afford to pay. Cat food's big money. What about the *Smithson Travel Agency*? Have they paid us what they owe us yet? It's been four months."

"Check for partial payment came in the mail yesterday." Lorna paused for a moment, a thoughtful frown crossing her features. "You could have them arrange it for you, you know."

"Arrange what?"

"A holiday. I wasn't kidding when I suggested that you need to take some time off. I can manage things here and I think you need a break. *Smithson Travel* owes us. They could probably get you a good deal on a package trip to Mexico or Hawaii."

Amalie looked at her partner. "I've been thinking about taking some time. Maybe going to the Caribbean."

"The Caribbean? That might be fun. Jamaica? Barbados?"

"I was thinking maybe St. Clement's."

"Never heard of it. Where and what is it?"

"I looked it up last night. It's sort of in the middle of nowhere. A tiny dot in a large sea." Amalie reached into her briefcase and pulled out the letter. She handed it to Lorna and watched silently as her partner read it.

Lorna frowned. "Do you suppose this is for real?"

"I don't know. I thought I might try to call her. At least that way I'll know whether she really exists and whether she's still alive. After all, even if the letter is the real thing, it was written five years ago and she was eighty then."

"Well what are you waiting for? Get on the phone and do it."

"Are you sure you can spare me?"

"No problem. Everything's up to date, and I can get someone in from the UCLA co-op program to do some of the grunt work while you're gone. We're only talking about three or four weeks aren't we? When was the last time you took a vacation? I go to Sun Valley skiing every year. You never take a holiday."

"I'll see if I can reach this Josephina Ansett. I guess that's the first step."

Amalie waited until after the morning session with the cat food account. Ronald Ainsworth, a delicate, fussy little man whose white side whiskers reminded Amalie of the cats for whom he produced food, was delighted with the ad campaign they'd put together for him. He left after approving all the plans and writing a sizable check.

Finally Amalie had no further excuse for procrastinating. Her hands were damp with tension as she picked up the phone and dialed the number on the letter. The phone rang only three times before it was picked up.

"Dis Elvirna. Who you wants?"

Oh dear, had she misdialed? Amalie spoke tentatively. "I'm sorry. I think I may have the wrong number. I was trying to contact a Miss Ansett."

"Why you didn't say? She right here."

A few moments later a surprisingly young voice came on the line. "This is Josephina Ansett."

Amalie paused for a moment and then plunged in. "Miss Ansett, you don't know me, but my name is Amalie Ansett. Five years ago you wrote a letter to my mother, inviting the two of us to visit you on the occasion of your eightieth birthday."

"Oh my dear child, how lovely of you to call. I always wondered why you and your mother didn't respond to my invitation."

"When it arrived my mother was very ill. She died a few weeks later. I found the invitation, unopened, among her things only now."

"I'm so sorry my dear. But you did find it and you have called. That means a great deal to me. I believe you and I may be the last of the Ansetts except for the British branch of the family. Is there any chance that you might be able to come see me here on St. Clement's?"

"Actually that's what I was calling about. I have some vacation time coming and I thought…"

21

"Why that would be wonderful. Please allow me to send you your air tickets."

"No. I assure you that's not necessary. I can have my travel agent arrange everything."

There was a tinkling laugh at the other end of the phone. "Good luck, my dear. Your travel agent won't even know where St. Clement's is. We're hardly a tourist destination and we're not very easy to get to. Tell him to get you as far as San Juan on any carrier. After that, it's a bit tricky. I recommend American Airlines to St. Luke's then you'll have to take AzurAir to St. Clement's. They're the only ones who come here. You'll have to overnight someplace, probably in Puerto Rico. If your agent has any trouble booking you on AzurAir, have him give me a call and I'll do it from here."

"Thanks, I'll do that. Can you book me into a hotel?"

Now the laugh was distinctly audible. "You'll stay with me. Don't worry. Ansett Beach House is really quite comfortable."

As she put the phone down, Amalie thought, what am I getting myself into?

CHAPTER 2

A week later, Amalie was on her way to St. Clement's. The trip was long, with stops in Miami and an overnight in Puerto Rico, but late in the afternoon of the second day of travel, she finally landed on St. Luke's. She found herself in a surprisingly modern airport. There were check-in counters for American Airlines, United, Continental, even Air France and Lufthansa, but nowhere did she see a sign for AzurAir.

She looked around, puzzled. Her flight was scheduled to leave in thirty minutes and she had no idea where her airline counter was.

"You on St. Luke's for holiday?" The speaker was a large well-dressed black woman. Her speech carried the distinctive trace of a British accent, but the rhythm and cadence, the unusual stress patterns, made it difficult for Amalie to understand.

"I beg your pardon?"

"I say you here for holiday on St. Luke's?"

"Oh. Yes. No. That is, I'm on a holiday, but I'm going to St. Clement's."

"What you goin' there for? Not even a hotel there. No place for a holiday."

"I have family there."

"Ah. Well, if you gets tired of doing nothin', come back here. Big hotels and casinos on St. Luke's. Lots of tourists comes to St. Luke's."

Amalie looked around her at the empty terminal building.

"Well, of course they's not here now. October. Hurricane season. Tourists, they comes in the winter."

"Hurricane season?"

"Almost over now. No worry. You come with me and I take you to AzurAir. You be wanderin' all over the place lookin'. They not by the other airlines."

"Why, thank you. I'd appreciate that."

They walked the length of the terminal building and around behind a shop selling duty free liquor to a small, almost hidden, booth. There Amalie's guide addressed an attractive middle-aged white man dressed in a crisp white shirt and blue trousers holding an unlit pipe clamped firmly between his teeth.

He smiled and spoke around the pipe. "Good Morning, Miss Eleanor. You keeping well?"

"Mornin', Pierre. No cause for complaint. This lady going to St. Clement's. You expectin' her?"

The man examined Amalie's ticket and consulted his passenger list. "Ansett." He looked at Amalie curiously. "Yes. She's on the manifest. Just take a seat over there, Miss Ansett." He waved airily

24

to a row of rickety benches. "We'll be leaving in about twenty minutes."

Amalie turned to her guide and smiled. "Thank you so much. I could have missed my flight while I was looking for AzurAir. And I'll remember what you said. If I want to get away from St. Clement's I'll head for St. Luke's. I'm Amalie Ansett." She shook the older woman's hand.

"Eleanor Johnston. Didn't know there was any Ansetts left on St. Clement's. Old family. Used to be lots of them." She gave Amalie a curious look. "You call me if you needs anything." The woman rummaged in her oversized purse, handed a business card to Amalie, then turned and strode away.

Amalie took a seat on the bench as the agent had instructed and examined the card. *Eleanor Johnston, Administrative Assistant, Office of the Governor.*

Amalie stared after the woman in surprise. Well, she thought. I seem to have made an influential friend. Smiling, she tucked the card in her carry-on.

Gradually, the bench beside her filled with other passengers, all some shade of black or brown. There was a very dark man with multiple gold chains around his neck and dreadlocks to his shoulders and a coffee colored woman with a large shopping bag filled with something that was moving. To Amalie's relief, a puppy stuck its head out of the top. There was a young light brown-skinned woman with two blue-eyed children in tow. Five passengers in all.

The man behind the desk put on a pilot's cap and came over to the bench. "Let's go."

The assembled passengers followed him out onto the tarmac, where a six-seater propeller plane of indeterminate vintage awaited. The pilot indicated that Amalie should sit beside him in the cockpit where a co-pilot normally would have been.

The take-off was smooth and soon they were flying over the cobalt blue of the sea. Puffy white clouds scuttled across the sky. Off to the left, a huge cone shape island jutted sharply up out of crashing surf.

"Saba", the pilot offered. "See that landing strip?"

Amalie looked down at a small patch of concrete cut cliff to cliff, halfway up the side of the mountain. "Is the landing at St. Clement's anything like that?" She hoped the fear wasn't evident in her voice.

The pilot chuckled. "The Saba landing's not as bad as it looks. But no, the St. Clement's strip is small, but it's on relatively flat land." He nodded toward the horizon. "There's your destination."

Amalie strained forward to catch her first glimpse of St. Clement's, its silhouette outlined against the sky. There appeared to be a high mountain on the left, with smaller, more rounded hills on the far right and a sort of saddle in between. As she watched, the shadowy form took shape as a lush verdant island.

"That large shape on your left is Mt. Zingara. It's an extinct volcano. You'll see the crater as we fly over it. Good hiking in there. Old mahogany trees. Vines. Even monkeys. But don't go up there alone. People get lost."

"Do you mean as in lost and not found?"

"Oh, no. They get found. But it means a lot of people have to stop what they're doing and go looking for the fools. It's a nuisance. Take a guide if you go."

"I'll remember that."

The pilot was silent for a few moments. Then he glanced at her. "Name on the manifest said Ansett. You related to Miss Josephina?"

"She's a distant cousin. I've never met her."

"She's a fine old lady." With that the box squawked and the pilot turned his attention fully to landing the plane.

The plane touched down smoothly and the pilot brought it around to stop directly in front of the small tin-roofed terminal building. Descending from the plane, Amalie followed the other passengers down a yellow brick path lined with oleander to a room crowded with people greeting each other boisterously, all laughing and talking at the same time. Amalie couldn't understand a word being said. She was wondering what she should do when a small form hurled itself at her.

"Oh my dear! I can't believe I wasn't here to greet you. We left the house as soon as we heard the plane. Andrew just doesn't drive as fast as he used to. It's the cataracts I guess. He refuses to get the operation and he doesn't see very well anymore. It makes him a bit cautious."

Amalie looked at the diminutive white haired woman before her and laughed out loud. "I take it you're my cousin, Josephina?"

"Of course I am. Who else would I be? And you are certainly Amalie. I'd have known you anywhere. Even if you hadn't been the only white face on the plane. Except for Pierre, of course. You look just like her."

"Her?" Amalie wondered if perhaps her cousin was just a bit dotty.

"Her. The other Amalie Ansett. But I'll tell you all about that later. Now you must be tired and hot and hungry. We'll fix that up, then we'll talk."

"I need to pick up my bag."

"Andrew is already doing that. It'll be in the jeep. Come, my dear. Let's go home."

Amalie followed Josephina out of the terminal building to the waiting vehicle.

"Andrew," Josephina said, "this is my cousin Amalie."

Amalie shook hands with an ancient, grizzle-haired black man.

"I'd have knowed her anyplace," he said, peering at her over thick glasses. "Welcome to St. Clement's, Miss Amalie. We is happy to have you here."

"Thank you. I'm looking forward to seeing your beautiful island."

Josephina took the front seat beside Andrew and indicated that Amalie should climb into the back.

"I have to sit beside Andrew to help him see," she explained.

The fifteen minute drive to their destination was hair-raising. It appeared that indeed Andrew could see very little. He drove at about fifteen miles an hour, squinting and peering over the steering wheel as Josephina kept up a steady stream of directions.

"Watch for that cow on the road!"

"Large pot-hole on your left."

"Car passing us."

Finally they turned off the road through an ornate wrought-iron gate and down a wide circular drive surrounded by hibiscus and frangipani. Andrew brought the vehicle to a stop in front of a modest two story yellow brick house, vaguely Georgian in style.

Giving silent thanks that they had miraculously reached their destination intact, Amalie turned to Andrew and suggested, "Why don't I take on the driving chores while I'm here?"

He smiled, relief written on his features. "I'd be obliged, Miss Amalie. I keep telling Miss Josephina I shouldn't be drivin', but she say she be my eyes. Not safe. I know it not safe."

Josephina led Amalie up the stone steps while Andrew followed with her bag. Wide double doors stood open to the tropical breezes welcoming them into a center hallway with doors opening to the right and left. At the back, a curving staircase led to a balcony surrounding the hall. Andrew started up the stairs with her bag as Amalie looked around.

The name, *Ansett Beach House*, had led her to expect something rustic, like the weathered clapboard beach houses she was used to on the west coast. This little jewel box of a house looked as if it had dropped out of eighteenth century England.

Josephina led Amalie upstairs to the room that would be hers. It was small but charming. An old fashioned mahogany four-poster had mosquito netting tied loosely in a knot above it.

Josephina chattered happily. "We aren't much bothered with mosquitoes. Generally the trade winds keep them away. But the netting can be useful occasionally, when the winds die down. And our electricity, I'm afraid, is a bit uncertain." She indicated the night table beside the bed on which sat both an electric lamp and a kerosene lantern. Then she nodded toward a doorway. "Your bath is through there."

Amalie was relieved to see that the bathroom was relatively modern.

"Our water supply is rainwater, stored in a cistern under the house. Sometimes the water pressure isn't very good," Josephina confided. "But if you just wait for a few minutes the pump will kick in and it will be fine." Josephina walked across to wide louvered doors on the far side of the bedroom and opened them. "But here's the best part."

Amalie followed her out onto a wide balcony that extended across the entire front if the house. Looking down, Amalie could see they were on a high promontory. Steps were cut into the rock face leading down to a bay where a wide black sand beach curved to another rock outcropping in the distance. Here and there stone ruins dotted the beach, the foundations of buildings from some distant past. Below her, the sea changed from turquoise to deep blue to a distant misty grey as it stretched to the horizon.

"It's beautiful," she breathed.

"I've always thought so. I'll leave you now to unpack and get settled in. I'm sure you'll want a shower and perhaps a little rest. We can reconvene at six o'clock for sundowners, if that's agreeable to you."

After unpacking, Amalie decided to lie down for just a few minutes. She didn't wake until seven o'clock. Embarrassed at being so late, she showered and dressed hurriedly, and rushed downstairs.

Josephina was sitting on the verandah. "I hope you had a good rest."

"I'm sorry to have slept so long. Why didn't you wake me?"

"You were clearly tired and we seldom eat dinner until well after sundown. Come and join me." Josephina indicated a second rocking chair beside her own. "Elvirna will bring us a rum punch then call us when dinner's ready."

"Elvirna? Is she the one I spoke to when I called you?"

"Indeed. She's Andrew's wife. Between them they've kept this place and me together for some forty years. I can't imagine what my life would be without them."

Over a dinner of locally caught grouper and baked plantains Josephina quizzed Amalie about her life in California. Amalie found herself confiding to Josephina's concern and interest more openly than she had to anyone since her mother's death. The story of her marriage and divorce, of the forced sale of her home, her feelings of displacement and anger all spilled out. Josephina listened with compassion and without comment except for an occasional, "Oh, my." or "Did he really do that?" or "That's too bad."

Somehow, at the end of her recital, Amalie felt better than she had in months.

That night she fell asleep to the sound of chirping crickets and piping tree frogs against the hypnotic percussion of the surf.

****

The crowing of a rooster directly under her window woke Amalie at dawn. She slipped into a pair of white shorts and a tee shirt. No one was about as she tiptoed down to the kitchen. Rummaging in the cupboards, she found instant coffee and made herself a cup.

Steaming cup in hand, she went out to the verandah and sat in one of the rocking chairs to watch the reflection of the sun paint the sea first mauve then rose. Tiny yellow birds, Bananaquits, chattered noisily as they flocked to take their breakfast from a hanging dish full of sugar, while brightly colored hummingbirds whirred at feeders. A blue-green lizard sat on the railing under the feeder, his tongue flicking out to lap up spilled over sugar. From the trees nearby she could hear the soft cooing of zenaida doves. A sense of peace washed over her such as she had not experienced in a very long time.

From the distance, a melancholy tune wafted up on the air. Someone was whistling. Amalie looked down the beach. A man walked at the edge of the waves. She could only see him from the back, but somehow, from the way he strode along, head down, shoulders slumped, hands clasped behind his back, she had the impression that he was not a happy man. His hair was long, tied loosely at the nape of his neck. She walked over to the railing to get a better view. He was dressed strangely for a walk on the beach. He wore a white shirt with billowing long sleeves and tight trousers tucked into knee high riding boots. He was walking in the surf with seeming unconcern for the waves splashing over his boots. The melody he whistled came to her clearly. She recognized it but couldn't at the moment name it or put words to it. It seemed so familiar. Something from her childhood perhaps?

As she stood staring at the man, pondering on the tune he was whistling, Josephina joined her.

"Good. I see you found the coffee. Elvirna will have breakfast ready in about a half hour. I usually have it out here." She indicated a small table and chairs at the far end of the veranda.

"That will be lovely." Amalie paused. "Who is that man on the beach?"

"What man?"

Amalie turned to where the beachcomber had been. No one was there.

"He must have gone around the headland at the other end of the beach. Although I don't know how he could have gotten that far so quickly."

"What did he look like?"

Josephina was quite still for a moment after Amalie described the man she had seen.

"Whistling, was he?"

"Yes. And I know the tune, but I just can't seem to remember what it is."

Josephina turned her back deliberately on the empty beach below. "I'm sure it was just a tourist. Let's go help Elvirna get the breakfast things on the table."

Amalie followed her into the kitchen. Why did she have the feeling that Josephina knew very well who the whistling man was?

Elvirna stood at a large old fashioned range turning cakes on a griddle. "Well, I see you not so tired this mornin'. You ready for some homemade johnnycakes with guava syrup?"

"That sounds heavenly."

Over breakfast Josephina regaled Amalie with amusing stories of island life.

Amalie asked about the rooster that had awakened her at dawn. "You're not keeping chickens, are you?"

"Not exactly. That would be Enrico."

"Enrico?"

"Enrico Carooster. Named for the famous tenor, of course. He's a most handsome fellow. He'll be here sometime during breakfast. He likes crumbs. But I do try to discourage him from coming up on the veranda."

Amalie laughed. "You have a pet rooster?"

"Not exactly. There are roosters and hens roaming free all over the island. This one just seems to have chosen to live with me."

"But how...?"

"It was about thirty years ago. Old Mr. Eustace decided to raise chickens and sell eggs. He took delivery of a hundred young chickens and for a while everything went according to plan. But in those days we were completely dependent for everything, flour, sugar, all basic supplies, on a boat, the Antillia, that came only once every six weeks. It was supposed to bring his chicken feed, but there came a time when it didn't. And then the next sailing, again it didn't bring any chicken feed. At that point Mr. Eustace opened the doors to his chicken coop and freed all his chickens to find their own dinner. They and their off-spring have been free ever since. They're all over the island."

Amalie shook her head in disbelief. It seemed another world.

As if in answer to his name, Enrico flew up to the railing and strutted over toward the table. Josephina held out some toast crumbs in the palm of her hand. The rooster nibbled at them delicately then stretched his wings wide, ruffled his neck feathers, thrust his head in the air, and crowed. Josephina scratched his chin and then shooed the colorful bird away.

"Off with you now!" Sitting back, Josephina changed the subject abruptly. "I thought you might enjoy a visit to the Historical Society Museum this morning."

Amalie looked at the sea spread out like an undulating blue carpet and thought how much she would rather spend the morning on the beach than any place indoors. A morning spent in a museum was not very appealing.

As if reading her thoughts, Josephina said, "You can go swimming after lunch if you like."

"Of course." Amalie reminded herself that she was, after all, Josephina's guest. A morning spent doing what her hostess wanted to do was a small thing. "Certainly I'd like to go to the museum with you. I can be ready to go in a few minutes. I'll drive."

"Excellent." Josephina stood up, and glanced at Amalie. "You'll have to change into either long pants or a skirt. Our local ladies take exception to shorts in town."

Amalie looked at her, puzzled. On the drive from the airport she had seen nothing she would remotely have identified as a town.

Reading her mind, Josephina said, "It's all in your frame of reference." Together they laughed and went indoors to change.

A half hour later they were in the little village. Low stone walls covered with lush bougainvillea edged the narrow cobblestone streets. Small clapboard houses were painted in rainbow colors, their roofs outlined in white gingerbread. The overall effect was reminiscent of a Victorian doll's village.

Turning a corner they came to a house much grander than any of the others. It sat in its own small park and, like Josephina's much smaller house, it was Georgian in style. Entirely constructed of yellow brick, it was fronted by wide semicircular stone steps, leading up to an impressive entranceway surrounded by white pillars.

"The Historical Society Museum," Josephina supplied. "It was built in the late seventeen hundreds and was the Governor's Mansion until just a few years ago. When the government decided that to build a more modern official residence, the Historical Society was allowed to take over this building. People from all over the island contributed to the displays."

Amalie studied the building. "It's made of yellow brick, like your house. I've never seen small yellow bricks like that before."

"A number of the older houses are built of that brick. It came here from Holland as ballast on the sailing ships in the sixteen hundreds when this island belonged to the Dutch."

The doors stood open. An attractive young woman whose café au lait skin seemed to have taken its golden hue from the sun itself sat behind a counter at the entrance.

"Good morning, Gustavia. I've brought a guest to see the museum. This is Amalie Ansett. Amalie, this is Gustavia Graham. Her family has been here on St. Clement's for more than three hundred years. We owe a number of these exhibits to the generosity of the Graham family."

Amalie smiled and extended her hand.

The woman looked at Amalie and for a moment seemed to pale. Then, recovering herself, she shook Amalie's hand and responded, "Nice to meet you, Miss Ansett."

Amalie followed Josephina through the anteroom to a large formal dining room. A highly polished mahogany table that could easily have seated twenty occupied most of the room while a large sideboard along one wall held an assortment of silver serving pieces.

Two formal oil portraits, one of a man, the other of a woman, hung over the sideboard.

"Governor Bradshaw and his wife Jane," Josephina explained. He was the first Governor of the island, from seventeen forty to seventeen fifty-nine. Later on the British made St. Luke's the seat of government and we had only an Administrator. But the Administrator always lived in the Governor's Mansion."

Amalie studied the two black clad, rather unyielding figures, staring down for all time at the table where doubtless they had entertained some two hundred and sixty years ago. What would their lives have been like here, so far from England?

Josephina continued through a door at one side of the dining room. "The kitchen," she said, indicating an assortment of rusted iron cooking utensils and a stack of pewter plates. "There would have been good English china of course. The pewter plates weren't for the guests, only for family. But not much of the china has survived. The few plates and serving pieces we've unearthed are in a glass showcase."

Amalie looked around. "But where did they cook? There's no stove, not even a fireplace."

"No one cooked in the main house in the tropics in those days. The cookhouse is outside. Come, I'll show you."

Josephina stepped out a doorway to a brick patio, on the other side of which was a small low ceilinged building.

"Food preparation and cooking happened here." Josephina pointed. "It was then carried into the serving kitchen."

Amalie stepped into the cookhouse. The ceiling was so low she could barely stand upright. Leaving the dark claustrophobic space she noticed a curved brick structure that looked almost tomb-like. It had a small iron door in one end.

"The bread oven," Josephina supplied.

Amalie shook her head. "It can't have been an easy life. They must have had a lot of servants."

"Not servants, my dear. Slaves. The Caribbean survived on slave labor for two hundred years. Slaves worked in the cane fields, slaves worked in the plantation houses, slaves maintained the lush gardens our ancestors wanted. Slaves were brought by the thousands to St. Clement's in unspeakable conditions in the holds of sailing ships. Those who survived the voyage were auctioned off on the beach right below my house or they were transshipped to North America. Slaves and sugar and rum were the basis of the economy here. It's not something of which we're proud."

Amalie looked at Josephina in shock. "I suppose I knew that on some level. I just never thought about it before."

"You're an Ansett and you have to understand where we came from. The people you'll meet on this island are almost all either descendants of slaves or descendants of slave owners. Or in most cases, such as with the young woman you met in the office just now, we're a mixture of the two. There was considerable mixing of the races over the years, inside and outside the marriage bed, both before and after the abolition of slavery."

The two women walked slowly back into the mansion.

Josephina hesitated. "There's one further thing I want you to see. It's why I brought you here this morning."

Puzzled, Amalie followed her into a drawing room furnished in eighteenth century style with a camelback sofa and wing chairs. Portraits lined the walls.

"Our past Administrators and their wives," Josephina commented as she walked across the room and looked up at one particular picture.

Amalie followed her gaze and gasped. She was looking at a portrait of herself.

"Amalie Ansett Benstone."

Amalie studied the image. It could have been her own. Of course the woman's clothing was different, and that other Amalie's ash blond hair was arranged formally in the long soft curls popular in that day rather than in the simple casual style today's Amalie preferred.

The woman in the picture appeared to be younger than Amalie by nine or ten years. She was perhaps eighteen. There was a softness about her face. It was gentle and sweet where Amalie's own features were a bit sharper, more defined. That was probably due to the fact

41

that she was older. However, there was one marked difference. Amalie Ansett Benstone's eyes were brown like her own, but they held no life. They were eyes that saw nothing.

"What happened to her? Why are her eyes so dead?"

"I'll tell you her story when we get back to the house. But first, perhaps you should look at the portrait of her husband, Charles Benstone. He was Island Administrator at the time."

Amalie looked at the picture beside her ancestor's. An involuntary shudder passed through her. It wasn't that Charles Benstone was unattractive. He was, in fact, extraordinarily handsome. High cheekbones accented an angular face. He was broad shouldered and powerful looking. His long black curly hair was carefully coiffed. However his mouth was shaped into a sardonic smile and his expression was arrogant, almost cruel. Looking at him, Amalie shivered again. How could a mere oil painting, and not very good one at that, make her feel such revulsion?

She turned to Josephina, questions churning.

"When we get back to the house," Josephina answered Amalie's unasked questions.

They made the trip back to Ansett Beach House in silence. Josephina didn't speak until they were seated on the verandah with steaming cups of herbal tea in front of them.

"I don't know the whole story. No one does. It's been handed down through the generations and I'm sure it's been embellished along the way. But the tale my great grandmother told is that Amalie was expected to marry Jonathan Evans. They'd been sweethearts since they were children and the match was approved of by both families. Among other things, their union would have joined the two greatest plantations on the island. Their properties combined cover the whole lower slope of Mt. Zingara on the leeward side of the island. You can drive out White Wall Road and see the ruins of the two adjoining plantations if you like."

Amalie nodded. "I'd like to do that. I didn't know there was any Ansett property other than this one on the island."

"Oh, my, yes. I still hold title to Ansett Plantation."

Josephina put her cup down and frowned in memory. "It was the night of the slave uprising."

"Slave uprising?"

"It was short lived. No one understood why the Evans Plantation was singled out. Jonathan Evans had the reputation of being a most benevolent owner. According to all written records, his slaves were well housed and well fed. They were looked after when they were sick. No one today can condone the practice of slavery, but there were owners who behaved kindly toward those on whom the whole economy of the island depended. And Jonathan Evans was one of them."

Amalie nodded, but a part of her wondered how anyone could make excuses for slavery, even in retrospect. She wasn't surprised that slaves rose up against their masters.

"It was the evening of December tenth, eighteen hundred and ten. Jonathan Evans was murdered and the plantation house was burned to the ground. Emile Ansett, Amalie's father, happened to be visiting at the time and he, too, was killed. A month later, Samuel, Jonathan Evans' man, was hanged for the atrocity, protesting his innocence."

The two women sat in silence for a few moments, sipping their tea.

"That's not the whole story is it?" Amalie said. "There's something more. Something that explains Amalie's dead expression in her portrait."

"Amalie married Benstone."

"That's understandable. After all, she was a young woman and however much she may have loved Jonathan Evans it was to be expected that she would marry someone else sooner or later."

"That's what's so very odd. It wasn't 'sooner or later'. According to island records, their wedding took place that same night. Amalie Ansett was in Government House being married at the time of the murders."

"With her father not there? With none of her family in attendance? That doesn't make sense."

"No, of course it doesn't. I suppose that's why the story has survived for all these years. It's a puzzle, a mystery that's never been solved."

"Perhaps Benstone persuaded her to elope. Swept her off her feet. Handsome men have been known to do that." Amalie thought of her own disastrous marriage. Brett had been devastatingly attractive.

Josephina looked into the distance. "Perhaps." She sighed. "Poor child. She didn't live for long. According to myth, she never spoke again after that horrendous night. Amalie Ansett Benstone lived only seven months longer. During that time it's rumored that she never indicated any awareness of her surroundings and she never uttered a sound, not even in the throes of childbirth. She died giving birth to a still-born daughter."

"I'm sure she must have been shocked at her father's and her former fiancé's fate. But never to speak again? Was she catatonic?"

"I suppose that's how it might be diagnosed today. In those days it was said she died of a broken heart."

"The portrait was painted after her marriage?"

"It was."

"That would explain the way she looks. What a horrible story."

The silence between the two women lengthened. Amalie thought, there must be more.

Then Josephina continued. "Of course, as with any good legend in the Caribbean, there's a ghost."

Amalie smiled. "You're not going to tell me that my namesake walks at night, scaring little children."

Josephina laughed aloud. "Of course not."

Amalie sat back, somehow relieved.

"It's not Amalie who walks, it's Jonathan. He's been seen a number of times over the years, walking down White Wall Road, whistling."

Amalie looked at Josephina to see if she was joking. Her face was devoid of expression as she picked up the tea cups and took them indoors.

Amalie continued to sit on the verandah for some time, staring at the sea, reliving the story she'd been told, thinking about the man she'd seen on the beach. Then she shook her head. What nonsense. Josephina had said he was probably a tourist.

What she needed was a swim. She stood to go indoors and change. At that moment, she heard the distant echo of whistling. She whirled to look down the length of the beach, but no one was there.

CHAPTER 3

The next days were spent exploring the island. Josephina delighted in taking Amalie to visit her friends, always introducing her as "my cousin from America." They sat drinking tea in the parlors of the tiny cottages in town that belonged to the older inhabitants and they sat drinking rum punch on the verandahs of large houses on the windward side of the island that belonged to expats who had settled there from the British Isles, America, and Europe. All welcomed Amalie with barely disguised curiosity. Visitors to St. Clement's were rare.

Amalie always drove while Josephina navigated. The roads were difficult. Many were unpaved and those that were paved were only one lane wide and full of potholes. Amalie became adept at pulling over into the bush when necessary to allow a vehicle coming the other way to pass. There seemed to be some unwritten rule about who pulled over and who took the road. Amalie couldn't quite figure out how the decision was made, but since it was as often in her favor as not, she didn't worry about it. The drivers of both vehicles used passing each other as an opportunity for conversation.

"Josephina, I've been meaning to have you and Amalie over for tea. Next Tuesday good?"

"Have you heard? Jennie Jamison has had her baby, a fine little boy."

"The fruit boat's in. They have some nice stems of bananas. You might want to check it out."

The result of these roadside chats was that it took a very long time to get from anyplace on the island to anyplace else. Amalie decided that there was clearly no need for a local newspaper. News was simply passed from car to car.

More dangerous than the roads themselves were the various forms of livestock, goats, sheep, cattle and donkeys, even occasional pigs, that wandered freely unattended and untethered.

"Are these animals all wild, like the chickens?"

"Oh my, no. They all belong to somebody or other. They have identifying marks on them, saying whose they are. It's just that when this island stopped being important, when the economy could no longer be supported on the backs of slaves, well, then there was all this land that used to be in plantations with nothing on it. It was just no longer necessary to fence animals in. They had free range of the island and nobody cared."

"But that was more than a hundred and fifty years ago. Surely it changed in recent years. There seem to be a lot of cars on the island now, and I've seen a number of very nice homes. There's very little evidence of farming here today. It doesn't appear to be an agrarian economy."

"No, it's not. There's very little farming. Things are changing. And the free roaming animals are a bit of a nuisance now, what with so many people having cars, and the animals a constant traffic hazard. But as you'll discover, things in the Caribbean change slowly. A man's wealth here is still measured by how many cows and goats he owns, even if he has a high paying government job and does nothing with his animals."

Amalie shook her head. There was so much here she didn't understand.

****

The time passed very agreeably. The two women established a routine by which they spent their mornings shopping, visiting Josephina's friends and sight-seeing together. Then in the afternoons Josephina would retire to her room while Amalie swam and sat on the beach reading from Josephina's extensive library of books about the Caribbean. At six, they met on the verandah to watch the sunset together with the traditional Caribbean rum punch before enjoying one of Elvirna's delicious dinners.

After dinner they played cribbage, a game Josephina insisted on teaching Amalie and which Josephina invariably won. During their game Amalie listened, entranced, as Josephina told her stories of the history of the island. About the old Ansett Plantation and the sugar cane and rum trade, the days when the now sleepy island had been a busy and prosperous place, a major port in the Caribbean. When the empty harbor had been filled with ships. Ships carrying St. Pierre's famous rum to northern ports, ships carrying armaments to the newly created American republic and slaving ships from Africa.

It all had a quality of unreality to Amalie, rather like the Greek myths and Grimm's fairy tales she'd enjoyed reading as a child.

Occasionally in the afternoon Amalie thought she heard that faintly disturbing whistled tune carried on the breeze and once while swimming she looked toward the beach and was sure she saw the man she had seen on that first day. His hand was up to shield his eyes and he seemed to be looking directly at her. But by the time she swam ashore he was gone.

****

"I think I should be making plans to return to California. I know I came with an open ticket, but it's mid-November. I've been here for six weeks now and I really shouldn't leave Lorna alone in the office much longer. We're coming into our busiest season."

Josephina looked distressed. "I had so hoped that having you here would..."

"Would?"

"I don't know. It's just that there's always been this mystery. And you look so much like her. I thought..."

"Josephina, I'm not that other Amalie Ansett. I have no way of solving your mystery. I wish I could, but what can I do that you or anyone else can't do?"

"I'm not sure. But the moment I saw you at the airport I had this feeling that finally everything would be put right. I can't explain it. It was just a feeling."

Amalie looked at Josephina. She was serious. Amalie knew at that moment that she did not want to disappoint this wonderful old lady who'd given her such a marvelous holiday. This cousin she'd never known before, for whom she had developed a great fondness. She had to try. She had to do something. But what?

"Perhaps I could stay a little longer. Are there are some archives I could look at?"

"Not really. There are boxes of old ledgers and papers in the museum, but nobody ever had time to sort through them."

"Would the museum give me permission to examine them?" Amalie didn't think for a moment there would be anything among a collection of old records that could solve Josephina's mystery but she felt compelled to try.

Josephina smiled. "Of course I can get you access to anything you want to see. I knew you'd help. I knew it the moment I saw you."

Amalie smiled at her cousin. The last place she wanted to spend the remaining days of her holiday was in the musty rooms of the museum, but maybe she could find something from those days that would shed light on…on what? On the hasty marriage, perhaps? That might be a matter of record. What had caused that other Amalie to break her engagement and so immediately marry another man?

"I'll see what I can discover. I'll spend the next few mornings there."

"Not tomorrow. It's Sunday and they won't be open. Besides there's someplace else I want to show you."

"I didn't think there was any place on this island we hadn't been in the last three weeks."

"White Wall Road. We haven't been out on White Wall. I want to show you Ansett Plantation, or at least what's left of Ansett Plantation."

The next morning Josephina directed Amalie through the town and out along a road that ran high above the sea between white cliffs on one side and the majestic green rise of Mt. Zingara on the other. The battered old green jeep lurched along the rough dirt road, past a few houses, then over a long wild stretch with no development. There wasn't even any electricity out here. The poles stopped at the edge of town.

"Why are there no houses out here?"

"Well for one thing there's no electricity."

Amalie glanced at her in disbelief. "Surely if people built homes out here electricity would follow?"

Josephina sighed. "It has to do with the jumbie. It's haunted and none of the locals want to move out here with a jumbie."

"Jumbie?"

"It's the West Indian word for the dead who walk. For ghosts."

Amalie glanced at her cousin to see if she was joking, but she seemed to be quite serious.

"The figure of a man roams the area at night. He whistles. He's been doing so for as long as anyone can remember. Nobody wants to live out here with a jumbie for company, even though he's never been known to harm anybody."

Amalie smiled and put the story down to the active imagination of the islanders, along with other stories she'd heard in the last few weeks about the old woman around back of the volcano who could work love spells, the mysterious crack in the Methodist church tower, and the woman who was buried standing up in the Anglican graveyard.

"When was the last time anyone actually saw or heard your jumbie?" she asked.

Josephina cocked her head to one side and frowned. "Mmm. My. It must be almost twenty years ago. A young courting couple walked out here for some privacy. It seems he actually spoke to them. They've been married for many years now, but they've never been back to White Wall. They were terrified."

"What is this ghost supposed to have said to them?"

53

"Their story never varies. A strangely dressed young man with blazing eyes approached them and said, *'Amalie, have you seen Amalie?'* Gerald, the young man, reached out to touch the man and encountered only air. He grabbed Esme by the hand and the two of them ran for their lives. They didn't stop until they were on the outskirts of town. That was the last time anyone reported seeing him, until…"

"Until?"

"Until you saw him on the beach."

"I saw him? I assure you I haven't seen any jumbies."

"Then who was the man you heard whistling on the beach? The one you described so clearly to me, dressed in what sounded like eighteenth century planter's clothing, right down to his boots. Who was that if not the ghost of Jonathan Evans?"

"Don't be ridiculous, Josephina. You surely don't believe these old wives tales? You can't really believe in ghosts. When I asked you about the man on the beach, you said he was a tourist."

"How many tourists have you seen on this island?"

"None, but I haven't seen any ghosts either."

As they talked the road had become rougher until it was little more than a dirt track. Clearly it was not much frequented.

"Here. Pull over here."

Amalie pulled the jeep to the side of the road beside an old stone archway.

54

"This is it. This is all that's left of the original wall and entrance to the grounds. We'd better change our shoes now. Sandals aren't a good idea when tramping through underbrush filled with cassia thorns and worse."

As they changed their sandals for runners, Amalie tried not to think about the *worse,*

centipedes and scorpions and possibly even snakes.

Following Josephina, Amalie pushed through the bush until they were standing in what must have been the entrance to the old manor house. There was no roof left, but high old stone walls remained standing even though there were trees growing up through the foundation and thick coralita vines covering everything. It was possible to see where windows had once been, outlined in curving brick. Flat, slave-cut stones lay in rubble around their feet.

Amalie remembered noticing a lithograph in Josephina's parlor. She hadn't realized when she looked at it that it was Ansett Plantation. The place had already started its decline at the time of the old photograph, but it was still standing then. It even had a roof of sorts.

Emotions churned through Amalie as she studied the ruin. Finally she said, "There is an aura of such sadness about this place."

Josephina nodded. "I thought you'd feel it. I've always felt it here. That's why I don't come very often. But I thought you should see it."

When Amalie went to the museum the next morning she was shown to a musty room in the basement. She looked in consternation at a solid wall of bookcases into which had been shoved box after box of papers, books, and ledgers with little or no attempt at categorization. She could spend the next year here and not make order out of this, let alone solve Josephina's mystery. Sighing, she pulled out the first box and set it on the wide pine plank table.

Four hours later, papers sorted into piles all over the table, she decided that was enough for one day.

She spoke to Gustavia before leaving. "I've left a number of papers on the table. Please don't let anyone touch them. I've spent all morning trying to get them into some kind of chronological order."

"Of course. Other than mine, there's only one key to that room and you may keep it while you're working on the papers. That way you can come any time you like."

As she walked out into the hot mid-day sun Amalie had a sudden desire to revisit Ansett Plantation. Somehow she wanted to see it on her own. She turned the jeep toward White Wall. Leaving the outskirts of town, she was struck once again by how empty of life this part of the island was. Even the goats and cattle and donkeys that wandered freely on all the other roads seemed to eschew this part of the island.

She pulled over at the old stone archway and made her way through the bush. Standing amidst the ruins, Amalie became momentarily disoriented. She swayed and grasped a wall for support as she was visited by a vivid memory of how it had been.

There, in place of the rubble, was a broad, generous house with wide verandahs and steps curving to the lawn. Bougainville climbed up the portal to the second floor, its coral and white flowers clambering over the veranda railings. On the main floor, tall windows glazed with panes shipped out from England, were framed by dark green louvered shutters designed to protect the precious glass from hurricane winds. It was early evening and the soft light of candles spilled through the windows. The scent of jasmine was strong in the air. The tinkling of an old fashioned pianoforte came from the drawing room. Behind the mansion as far as the eye could see up the slopes of the volcano, fields covered with sugar cane rustled in the breeze.

Slowly the vision faded. Only the distant echo of music and the faint scent of jasmine lingered. Then they too were gone. How could she so clearly remember what she had never seen? Amalie shivered in the now eerie silence, chilled, her arms in covered in goose bumps.

A deep male voice startled her. "It was a beautiful place."

Amalie turned toward the voice. With some effort she shook off the past. It was the man from the beach. How had he gotten here without her hearing him?

She stared at him. "Who are you? How did you get here?"

He was dressed as before, in a full sleeved shirt open at the neck and pants tucked into knee high leather riding boots. He carried a wide brimmed planter's hat in his hands. He was attractive, but not picture book handsome. His sandy colored hair was long, pulled back and fastened at the nape of his neck and his eyes were a deep piercing blue with laugh lines at the corners.

"I often walk on this road." He had a wide, generous mouth which at this moment was tilted in a lopsided smile. "I didn't mean to frighten you."

Amalie drew herself up to her full five foot seven. Frightened, indeed! She looked up at him defiantly. "You didn't frighten me. I was just surprised to see you here. I thought I was alone."

"Do you mind the company?"

"No. No, of course not." She paused then added, "I've seen you before. You like walking on the beach. Josephina tried to persuade me that you were a jumbie. I'm glad to meet you in the flesh."

"And I've seen you often. You like swimming in the afternoons."

Amalie looked toward the road. "It's a long walk back to town. Can I give you a lift?"

"A lift?" He looked puzzled.

"A lift. A ride back into town?"

He looked toward the jeep parked by the side of the road. "That might be interesting. I've never been in a mode of transportation quite like yours."

Amalie laughed. "It is a pretty decrepit vehicle."

They walked together back to the jeep. The man watched with interest as Amalie put the key into the ignition and brought the motor to life then pulled efficiently out of the deep grass onto the dirt track.

"You do that very well. Do you also ride?"

"You mean as in ride horses?"

"Yes, ride. Horseback."

"No. I lived in cities all my life. I never had the opportunity to learn."

"Pity. Somehow I was sure you would ride."

They sat in silence for a moment. As they bumped along the road Amalie thought about Ansett House and the period when it had been so filled with life. Then reality pushed into her fantasy.

"I know it was at one time a beautiful house, but those cane fields were worked by slaves," Amalie said. "My cousin told me how cane had to be harvested and turned by hard slave labor into molasses and rum in the Evans distillery."

"That's true. Ansett and Evans Plantations were both a part of the triangle that all Caribbean merchants and plantation owners were engaged in. The slave trade. Slaves to molasses to rum."

The day was hot, but again a chill passed across Amalie's shoulders. "It's horrible to contemplate."

"It was another time. And there were kind owners. Owners who saw to it that their slaves were well fed and housed, who never beat them or sold them away from their families. After all, slaves represented a major financial investment. It just made sense to look after them."

Amalie frowned. "Are you defending the practice of slavery?"

"No. I know it was morally wrong. But you must remember it was a way of life here for more than two hundred years. People knew no other way. Most planters were born into a world where there were slaves and there were masters. And most felt some level of responsibility for the well-being of their slaves."

"How can you possibly know that? And how is it that you know so much about the history of St. Clement's? I thought you were a stranger here."

"Oh, no. What gave you that idea? I'm no stranger to this island. And I do know for a fact that some slave owners were kind and some weren't."

Amalie noticed he hadn't answered her question about how he knew, but before she could rephrase her question, he spoke again.

"We're approaching the outskirts of town. I'd best get out here."

"Sure." Amalie pulled the vehicle to the curb.

He jumped out and turned to her. "Thanks for the ride. It was most informative."

"Wait," she called after him. "You haven't told me your name. Where are you staying?"

But he seemed not to hear as he strode down a side lane and disappeared around the corner.

Amalie became aware that people were staring at her. A man walking along the side of the road stopped in his tracks. A woman who had been sitting on her front steps stood and peered at her. Two children playing a game in a dusty front yard looked up at her and then ran away. What was wrong with them? After all she just wanted to know who he was. Perhaps she shouldn't have called after his retreating figure. It wasn't very lady-like. And this island was quite old fashioned in some ways.

But who was he? And how was it that on all her visits to households around the island she'd never once come across him? He was no ghost, whatever Josephina thought. Amalie's mind wrestled with the problem as she drove back to the beach house.

The first words out of her mouth when she was seated on the veranda with Josephina were, "I've met your ghost. I can assure you he's as real as you or I."

"Is that so? How very interesting. Where did you meet him? And who is he, if he's not our ghost?"

"I met him at Ansett Plantation. I drove out there today when I finished at the museum."

"What's his name?"

Amalie squirmed. "I didn't quite get his name."

"I see. He didn't mention his name." Josephina smiled in an annoyingly knowing way.

"No, he didn't." Amalie bristled. "We got involved in conversation. We talked about the reliance on slave labor here in the old days. Josephina, when were the slaves freed on this island?"

"Well, the slave trade was abolished in eighteen hundred and seven. That is the buying of slaves in Africa and transporting them for sale to plantation owners here and on other English islands was made illegal. But the slaves already here in the British West Indies weren't actually freed until much later. Not until the Act of Emancipation in eighteen forty."

"You mean that slavery continued on these islands for another thirty-three years after the abolition of the slave trade?"

"I'm afraid so. And the Act of Abolition merely pushed the slave trade underground. It became a way for the traders to make even more money. The price for a good strong man more than doubled. Slave smuggling brought huge profits. And since the slaving ships had to be smaller, lighter and faster than the patrol ships, the conditions in which slaves were transported were even worse than they had been before."

"You seem to know a great deal about this."

"It's my family history. Yours, too. You need to know these things, Amalie. You're an Ansett."

"What happened when the slaves were finally freed? What happened to all those men, women, and children who used to work on the plantations?"

"The government gave them land. Most found they could live comfortably with a just a small piece of land to farm and a few animals. Some went to the larger islands of course. None wanted to continue working on the sugar plantations, not even for money. It was backbreaking work and money was a commodity they were used to doing without."

"And the plantations? How did they survive without slaves to do the work?"

"In the long run most didn't survive. Some owners turned to other crops. They fared best. Others brought in workers from elsewhere, India, Indonesia, China. Some tried bringing in indentured servants from Great Britain. None of that seemed to work very well. Work on a sugar cane plantation was killing work. Gradually the sources for workers dried up and the plantations fell into decay."

"And the owners?"

"Most of them left. They returned to England. They became absentee landlords and the islands became essentially the property of the former slaves. There are only a few of the old plantation families left here on St. Clement's still holding on to their land. I'm the last of the Caribbean Ansetts."

Elvirna appeared in the doorway. "You two goin' sit here all night talkin'? Dinner's ready an' gettin' cold."

Josephina glanced at her watch. "I had no idea it was so late. Sorry, Elvirna. You can bring it out now."

"I'll come help." Amalie walked back through the house with Elvirna to the kitchen and the housekeeper started dishing out the fragrant fish stew that was tonight's dinner.

"Heard you talking to Miss Josephina 'bout the jumbie."

"Jumbie?"

"Don't make as you don't know. The jumbie. The ghost of Jonathan Evans."

"Don't be ridiculous, Elvirna. You know there's no such thing as jumbies. I met a man. A real live man. As real as you or I."

"And he just appear out of nowhere and then he just disappear back into nowhere. Wake up girl. He wants somethin' from you. You is named Amalie. You looks like that other Amalie. You done bring him back."

"That's the silliest thing I ever heard in my life." Amalie took the two bowls of steaming stew out to the veranda. She could feel Elvirna's eyes boring into her back as she left the kitchen.

The next morning she returned to the museum to resume her work. When she entered the small basement room she found the

64

papers she'd left on the table scattered all over the place. They were no longer in tidy piles according to date and type of document. It was as if someone had been looking for something and hadn't cared how much mess they made.

Amalie stormed upstairs and found Gustavia sitting behind her desk.

"Who got into the archives overnight?"

Gustavia looked up, startled. "No one. You have the only key except for mine and I keep all the museum keys with me. Nobody else had access to that room."

"Well somebody was in there. And they undid the solid morning's work I put in yesterday."

Gustavia frowned. "I can't imagine how that could have happened."

Amalie shook her head. "I can fix them up again. It's just maddening. Obviously someone was looking for something. But why now? After all, those papers have been around for a long time. Anyone who wanted something from them has had years to find it. Why now, when I've just begun to look at them?"

"I don't know. Perhaps it's because you've started to look at them. But that doesn't answer the question about the key. I suppose there might be another one floating around somewhere. After all I only took over here five years ago. I thought all the keys were turned over to me, but…"

Amalie sighed. "That must be the answer. Sorry for jumping all over you. I was just annoyed to see the mess. I'd better get back to it if I'm going to accomplish anything today."

In the basement room, Amalie contemplated the papers strewn around the wide pine table. There was a large, leather-bound ledger sitting on top of them. She hadn't noticed that yesterday. Where had it come from? She opened it and started to read the faded ink entries.

To her shock she discovered it was a ledger of slave sales, with descriptions and prices.

1 male and 2 females, household slaves to Jeremiah Johnston ....
425 guineas.

2 field workers to Emerson Gainsborough.... 250 guineas

6 field workers to John Taylor.... 1250 guineas

The room spun around her. She grasped the edge of the table to keep from falling as consciousness faded.

She was in a harbor full of wooden ships. A crowd of men, from the look of their clothing, planters, shopkeepers and businessmen, milled about the dock, shouting to one another, pushing and shoving, vying for position. The cacophony was ear splitting. A large vessel was pulled up to the pier. Naked male slaves, their ankles chained together, were shuffling down the gangplank and being herded into a holding pen. The smell of their fear and hopelessness hovered in the air.

Amalie heard a voice raised above the clamor and turned to see an auction block.

"And here we have a fine specimen from the Gold Coast. You all know there ain't no stronger or better field workers than these. Turn around, boy. Let'em see you. So what am I bid? Come on gentleman."

Bids started coming, fast and furious.

Horrified, Amalie watched as the young man was led away by the successful bidder.

When she turned back to the auction block she saw that it was occupied by an emaciated boy barely into his teens. Even in the hot tropical sun he stood shivering as the crowd jeered and the auctioneer turned him around for prospective buyers to examine.

"I'll admit he ain't much, but he might be some use as kitchen help. Don't know how he got into this batch. Was supposed to be all field workers. What am I bid? Come on gentlemen, got to move along. Don't nobody want this scrawny piece o' nigger flesh?"

There was a moment's silence. Then from the back of the crowd, near where Amalie stood invisibly, "I'll take him. Ten guineas." The speaker was a boy no older than the one on the block.

"Ten guineas?" the auctioneer sneered. "Might as well give 'im away. What am I bid, gentlemen?"

The crowd was silent. The boy reached into his pocket and counted out a handful of change. "Ten guineas and twelve bob."

Someone in the crowd called out. "Jonathan Evans. Your pappy know how you're squanderin' his money?"

The crowd broke into raucous laughter.

"Never you mind." The auctioneer took control. "The boy's money's as good as anybody else's. You got yourself a slave, boy. Come and git him."

Amalie was back in the basement room, her head on the table. What had just happened? She must have fallen asleep. It was a horrible dream. But it had seemed so real. She shook her head to clear the cobwebs

She looked down at the ledger in front of her.

One boy, sold to Jonathan Evans for 10 guineas and 12 pence, 15 August 1795.

"That's it. I need some fresh air."

She hastily locked the door and made her way up the stairs.

Gustavia looked up as she came into the room. "I was wondering if I should go down and check on you. You've been working a long time."

Amalie glanced at her watch and realized that it was well after two. She'd been in that basement room for hours. Josephina must have wondered why she hadn't come home for lunch.

"I guess I lost track of the time."

When she stepped out into the blinding sun she took a deep breath and looked around her. There was just enough breeze to keep it from being really hot. Birds were chirping in the trees. Cars drove by on the road in front of the museum. People called greetings to each other in passing. Everything was blessedly normal.

What she needed was a swim and a nap. Well, perhaps not a nap. She didn't need any more dreams like that one. It must have been that ledger entry that set off her active imagination. Still, where had the ledger come from? She hadn't put it on the table. She was almost sure she hadn't. Had someone wanted her to see that particular entry? The one with Jonathan Evans' name in it?

****

"How's the holiday going?" Lorna asked late that afternoon when Amalie answered her phone.

"It's proving to be a very interesting experience."

"Oh?"

"Well, I love my cousin Josephina. She's a delight. At times she seems rather odd and, I don't know, sort of a bit fey. And then at other times I see this incredible intelligence and knowledge shining through. She's altogether wonderful and I'm so glad I've found her."

"It's good that you feel you have family again. But I thought you'd be back long before this. You must be having a really good time."

"Part of it's that. I swim every day. The water's wonderful, clear and warm. And I must have gained five pounds. Elvirna, my cousin's cook, is magic in the kitchen."

"You said, part of it. What's the other part? Don't tell me you've found a man?"

"No. No, certainly not." What could she say to Lorna? She wasn't sure she even understood herself what was holding her here. "It's just that there's this mystery surrounding the other Amalie."

"The other Amalie?"

Amalie hurried on before she lost the courage to say what even to her sounded crazy. "My distant ancestor. Her picture's in the museum here, and, well, we do look very alike and Josephina seems to think I can unravel some of the mystery surrounding her broken engagement, hasty marriage, and death."

There was a moment's silence on the other end of the line. Then, "That seems a rather tall order. How long ago did this other Amalie die?"

"Some two hundred years or so."

"And your cousin thinks you can unravel a mystery that old?"

"I know how it sounds. But yes, she does. And I feel I have to at least try. In all honesty, I want to try. Somehow her story intrigues me."

"Well, I'm managing here without you. But don't stay too long. You're the one with the artistic talent in this partnership. I need you."

"Only a couple more weeks. I should either find something by then or know that there's nothing to be found."

"Let me know if I can do anything to help from here. I miss you, Amalie."

"And I miss you, Lorna. I wish you could be here. This place is magic. It's like stepping into some kind of time warp. I could easily get used to living here."

Lorna's warm laugh floated over the line. "Don't do that. I have no desire to look for another partner."

After she had put her cell phone down, Amalie sat staring into space. It was true. She would enjoy living here. Her entire life she'd been surrounded by the noise and confusion of cities. She'd always considered herself to be a modern woman, capable in the world of business, happiest when under pressure to perform. Motivated by the desire to make a name for herself, to make money, to get ahead.

And yet here she'd fallen so easily into the routine of slow mornings followed by lazy afternoons capped by a sunset rum punch with Josephina and one of Elvirna's spectacular dinners. Evenings of losing at cribbage as she listened to Josephina's tales of the history and myth of St. Clement's. She could never have anticipated the way in which this place would take hold of her. Very simply she loved it. It felt like home to her.

Shrugging off her thoughts, she went downstairs to join Josephina.

Chapter 4

It happened two days after Lorna's call. Amalie had come down to the kitchen early, as was her custom, so that she could enjoy her first cup of coffee in solitude. She stepped out to the veranda and almost dropped her cup when she saw Josephina's rocking chair occupied.

"What are you doing here? Where did you come from? And who are you?"

"Good morning to you, too. Please join me. I've always loved this time of day." The man from the beach turned his slow lazy smile on her.

Amalie laughed. "Good morning. I'm sorry. It's just that you startled me. It's all that nonsense Elvirna keeps talking about jumbies. I wasn't expecting you to be here."

His face turned serious. "I thought it was time we talked."

Amalie examined the man sitting beside her. He looked normal, whatever normal was. Attractive. Not the pretty boy looks of her ex-husband, but a sort of rugged handsomeness. Skin tanned by seasons in the sun. His midnight blue eyes had captured her from the moment she first saw him out at Ansett Plantation.

73

She spoke sternly. "Good. Start with who are you and why you're here. I get the odd feeling this is some sort of game you're playing, a game that could have serious consequences. You've been following me, watching me. You said as much yesterday."

His looked at her for a long moment. Amalie felt almost seared by his hypnotic gaze. "You know who and what I am, Amalie. Why are you afraid to admit that you know me?"

Amalie shivered. "It's not possible. I don't believe in ghosts or jumbies or whatever you think you are. This has gone on long enough. You're as alive as I am. I can see you, I can hear you, I can touch you." To prove her point, Amalie put her hand on his arm and jerked it back as if it had been burned. She drew in her breath sharply. Her hand had gone straight through his arm to the wood of the arm rest.

"I'm Jonathan Evans, Amalie. You know me. As to why I'm still here after two hundred years, I have no idea. I don't know what went wrong on that night, what happened or how it happened. I only know I was alive and now I'm not."

"No. It can't be," she murmured. Was she losing her mind? Still, she couldn't touch him. How could that be?

"I'm a ghost, Amalie," he said, as if reading her mind. "A jumbie, a spirit. Not a figment of your imagination."

Amalie shook her head. "Why me? You said two hundred years. Assuming I believe what you say, that you're from the spirit world, why me?"

"We were betrothed, you and I, Amalie. We were wed briefly. I loved you then and I love you now. You're my Amalie. I've been waiting for you for so long and now you're here. You can see me and hear me in a way no one else has in all that time. There has to be some reason for that. I think we're together again for some purpose. Together perhaps we can put what went so wrong two hundred years ago, right."

"Jonathan, even assuming you're who you say you are, I'm not your Amalie. That was another time and another person. I don't see how I can help you."

The screen door slammed as Elvirna came out to veranda, her hands full of plates and cutlery. "You talkin' to that pesky rooster? Don't know why Miss Josephina puts up with him."

Amalie whirled to the chair beside her. It was empty, still moving gently. And Josephina's pet rooster was indeed on the railing, strutting toward her.

Jonathan Evans was real. True she couldn't touch him. She had a fleeting thought that it was a pity. She would rather have liked to touch him. But how could she help him? She wasn't that other

Amalie, no matter what he thought. She couldn't be, could she? And yet where had those memories of Ansett Plantation come from?

Josephina arrived at the table for breakfast at that moment and all thoughts of ghosts had to be put aside.

"What are your plans for the day, my dear?"

"I'll spend the morning working in the archives again then this afternoon I guess I'll just swim and read as usual."

"Could you run me up to town before you begin? I need to see my solicitor."

"Of course."

It was mid-morning when Amalie entered the basement room at the museum.

"You!" Amalie looked at Jonathan, perched on her stool, his hair falling over his forehead, his elbows on the table, his long legs stretched out in front of him. He was whistling softly. That same elusive tune.

"You're rather late getting here. I've been searching for evidence."

She stared at him. He looked so real, so alive.

Reading her thoughts he said, "Jonathan Evans, in the flesh. Except that, unfortunately, I'm not in the flesh. If I were I could kiss you as I should very much like to."

Amalie flushed. The thought of being held in those arms, caressed, kissed by those lips…she turned her thoughts hastily away from that direction.

"What's that tune you're always whistling?"

"Greensleeves." He sang a phrase, his voice low and melodious.

"Alas, my love, you do me wrong,
To cast me off discourteously,"

He sighed. "You used to sing it."

"I used to sing it?"

"You used to sing it."

"It must have been the other Amalie who sang it. But I know it from somewhere. I'm not sure where." She finished the stanza in her light soprano,

"While I have loved you well and long,
Delighting in your company…"

Jonathan looked long at her. "Of course you know it. You are one with her. Why do you find this so hard to accept?"

Amalie just shook her head. How could she possibly be a woman who died two hundred years ago? She was alive. She was born in the twentieth century. For that matter, how could she possibly be holding this ridiculous conversation with a ghost?

Jonathan looked back down at the table, changing the subject. "Did you see the ledger I left on the table for you yesterday?"

"You were the one who messed up my piles of papers? I should have known."

"Did you look at the entries?"

Amalie remembered. "There was an auction. Somehow, I was there. You were just a young boy. And you bought a boy about your own age. How could you have done that?"

"Samuel. Would you rather he'd been bought by someone who'd have put him in the fields? He'd have died within a year. I took him home with me. I made him my valet. When I had lessons with my tutor, Samuel sat beside me. He learned to read and write and do figures. We rode together, fished together, swam together. He may have been a slave, but he was my friend. My only friend. And when my father died and I inherited the plantation at the age of twenty-one, I freed Samuel. It was my first act as owner. He became my estate manager. He chose to stay with me, but he was a free man."

"I'm sorry. There's just so much I don't know. Don't understand."

Jonathan pushed a yellowed British newspaper across to Amalie. "And Samuel, who would gladly have given his life for me, is the man newspaper accounts of the day say murdered me and led a slave revolt."

Amalie took the paper and swiftly scanned the story. It was largely as Josephina had recounted it to her. Yet everything Jonathan said had the ring of truth. If Samuel was indeed free, why would he have turned against his benefactor?

"No. It doesn't make sense. But how do you think we can untangle a two hundred year old mystery with nothing but a bunch of musty old files to guide us?"

Jonathan sighed. "I don't suppose we can. Let's get out of here. I need to walk and think."

****

"Has there ever been any suggestion that it may not have been the slave, Samuel, who killed Jonathan Evans and Emile Ansett and burned down the plantation?" Amalie asked Josephina later that day.

"You've found something in the archives, haven't you? I knew you would."

"Not really. At least not anything that would hold up as evidence." Amalie had a sudden image of trying to convince people of what she had been told by a ghost. "But some things just don't hold together, as reported."

"Such as?"

"Did you know that Samuel wasn't a slave? That Jonathan Evans had freed him eight years before the murder?"

"No. In all the accounts I've heard, he was referred to as a slave."

"He was a free man, and devoted to Jonathan. Certainly not the most logical candidate for a murderer."

"I always knew there was more to this story than met the eye. And I knew you would be the one to uncover it."

Amalie hoped her cousin was right.

The next morning when Amalie came out to the veranda with her coffee, Jonathan was there waiting for her.

"Let's walk."

As they strolled on the beach Amalie turned to him and asked, "What was it like growing up here all those years ago? Did your parents send you away to school? I've heard that was quite usual in those days."

"No. My mother died giving birth to me. I was an only child and my father was reluctant to have me out of his sight. I ran wild as a youngster, unrestrained by any of the slaves whose job it was to look after me. One particular woman, Kishima, was like a mother to me. She was the one who fixed up my banged knees and dried my tears and fed me sweets. I loved her."

"What happened to her?"

His face hardened. "She was killed in an accident in the boiling house when I was ten. I'd rather not talk about it."

They stood looking at each other. His eyes were bleak. Amalie wished she could find some way to comfort him, but how did one comfort a ghost?

"It doesn't sound like much of a childhood," she ventured.

They walked on in silence for a few moments then Jonathan started speaking again. "Once I was past my earliest years, my father hired a tutor whose responsibility it was to turn me from the young savage I was into something approaching a civilized man. He was a Jesuit and a scholar, although I'm not sure I fully appreciated that at the time. I studied Greek and Latin and mathematics with him. He was a good man, a severe taskmaster, but always fair. He remained my friend for the rest of my life."

"You must have been very lonely, with no mother and no brothers and sisters."

"That's why Samuel was so important to me. I don't know what took me to the slave auction that day. But it was one of the luckiest days of my life. From the time I first took him home with me, Samuel was my constant companion. We did all the things boys do together." He laughed in sudden recollection.

"Once, when we were exploring the rainforest in the crater of Mt. Zingara, we caught an iguana. It must have been five feet long. Somehow we got it home, wriggling and objecting all the way, and put it in a cage overnight. The next morning it looked so forlorn that we let it go. You have no idea how fast those reptiles can run when they want to. It was quite a sight."

Amalie smiled at the mental image of the two boys, one black and one white, hovering over a cage and releasing the hapless creature.

81

Jonathan continued. "Samuel sat beside me when I had my lessons, learning along with me. Brother Xavier ignored Samuel, but never objected to his presence."

After that first day, Amalie became accustomed to finding Jonathan waiting for her when she came down each morning. They made a habit of walking on the beach before the household was stirring. As they walked they told each other about their lives, his in the eighteenth century, hers in the twenty-first. Sometimes they discussed quite inconsequential things.

"So you work in this place called Los Angeles. The Angels. You say it's a big city. I went to London once so I think I know what that means. But I don't understand what it is that you do. You work? You *advertise*?"

"Yes. I try to sell my client's businesses to the public. They hire me to help them sell their products."

"What kind of products?"

"Well, just before I came here I was working on a cat food account."

"Special food for cats? You were trying to sell that? Incredible!"

Amalie proceeded to describe both the advertising campaign for *PURR* cat food and the eccentric owner of the cat food company.

Jonathan threw back his head and roared with laughter. "You made that up."

"No. I swear it's true. Suddenly Amalie saw the absurdity of her life. She was trying to make sense to someone from the eighteenth century something that was basically silly even in the twenty-first.

She started laughing uncontrollably, reached out unconsciously to Jonathan and felt him beneath her hand. He did not have quite the solidity of flesh, but he was no longer merely air.

Shocked, they both stopped laughing and stared at each other.

"I have felt myself becoming more real, more complete, day by day, since you first arrived."

"How can that be?"

"How can any of this be?"

He reached toward her and kissed her lips, a gentle kiss, no stronger than a breeze, but Amalie felt it to the depth of her being. This couldn't be happening. She could not be falling in love with a ghost. Worse yet, a ghost who thought she was someone else, an ancestor who had lived some two hundred years ago.

After that, when they walked, Amalie often leaned against Jonathan, taking comfort in the increasing solidity of his presence, his arm draped casually around her shoulder. He always greeted her with a lingering kiss and the more she was with him, the more deeply entangled her feelings toward him became.

One morning she asked him about the other Amalie.

"How can you not remember? We were inseparable from the time we met. You were just fourteen, and you used to slip away to meet me at the beach. There's a special spot below the rocks that can't be seen from the houses or fields. It was our special meeting place." Jonathan stopped and turned toward Amalie. "We became lovers there when you were just sixteen. You must remember that."

Amalie shook her head in denial. "It wasn't me, Jonathan. It was that other Amalie, the one who lived in your time."

"You are one and the same. I don't understand how that can be, but I know it to be true. You're the one I've been waiting for. You're the one I've always loved. I cannot be wrong about that. There is so much I'm unsure of, but of that fact I'm certain."

Then one day he spoke to her of an event that changed his life.

"It was my twelfth birthday. It was the time of year for the cutting and processing of the cane. Until then I had never been allowed inside the boiling house. It was an impressive building. From the distance you might almost have thought it was a church with its massive chimney reaching to the sky like a steeple. But what was inside was no church. I knew the slaves dreaded and feared what happened in there, but I was never aware of why. On that particular day my father took me in to see it all. There were three catwalks. We stood on the highest, just under the roof. On the floor massive vats were seething and bubbling over huge fires, like the very fires of hell. The heat, even where we stood, was unbearable and the overpoweringly sweet, sickening stench of molasses nauseated me.

The slaves were on the lowest catwalk, working naked, men, women and children."

He paused and shook his head. "I don't know how they could breathe. It was their job to use wooden paddles to stir the vats and to keep the thick molten sugar moving along toward huge gutters that ran toward cooling vats on the other side of the factory. On the middle level catwalk were the white drivers. They usually oversaw the work in the fields, but here they wielded long whips and they kept flicking them on the helpless slaves below to keep the up the pace of the work."

Amalie turned to him, caught up in his story. "What did you do?"

"What could I do? I was just a boy. My father was so proud of the whole thing. And I hated it. When we got back outside I was wretchedly sick. My father watched with amusement as I threw up. He told me I would get used to it. That I had to get used to it because it was our way of life. That our livelihood depended upon it."

Amalie shuddered. "I had no idea."

"Nor had I, and I had lived in the shadow of that purgatory my whole life. I swore that if I ever had the opportunity I would shut down the mill forever. Of course I didn't say that to my father. He would never have understood. But I did talk to Brother Xavier about it."

"What did he say?"

"He put the anti-slavery writings of Clarkson and Wilberforce into my hands. After reading what they had to say, I determined that if ever I was in a position to do so I would free our slaves. And that whatever else happened I would turn to other crops. Crops that could be harvested in a less dehumanizing way. I would never again grow cane."

"And were you able to do that?"

"I was in the process of doing that when…when everything stopped."

Each time they talked Jonathan's world seemed more real to Amalie. As he talked, his past came alive.

"It was wonderful growing up here. There is a special fragrance to these islands —can't you smell it? A mixture of spice and tropical plants." He gestured toward the shoreline. "The lushness of the foliage, the shades of green of the land and the turquoise and blue of the sea. And of course the constant freshness of the trade winds. It always seemed to me a small slice of paradise. And once I found you, my world was complete. There could have been no better place on earth."

He pulled her close to her and held her in an embrace that was soft as clouds. Amalie rested her head on his shoulder.

She loved the sound of his voice, deep and melodious, the ring of his laughter when she said something he found amusing and the way his eyes crinkled when he laughed. On those rare mornings when he didn't appear, she found herself quite disappointed.

One day when they were walking he stopped and turned her to him. "You didn't sleep well last night."

"How do you know that?"

"You cannot always see me when I'm there. I've been watching you sleep for weeks now. It gives me great comfort."

That night when Amalie climbed into her bed she said, "Jonathan?"

"Yes?" He appeared, sitting in her armchair, relaxed, his legs crossed at the ankles.

"Come lie with me. I would have your arms about me as I sleep."

She slept well that night, in an amorphous embrace.

It was two nights later that she awoke in the middle of the night. Her nipples were rising to hard points as soft air brushed over her, silken and caressing.

"Yes," she whispered.

"Are you sure?"

"I'm sure." She knew she'd been waiting for this moment. Perhaps all her life.

Jonathan's hands seemed to have a magic of their own as they explored her body, lightly touching yet not touching, arousing wherever they hovered, her face, her throat, her breasts, her stomach

87

and, shockingly, between her legs, brushing her sex and bringing her to frenzy. His lips, feather light, followed his hands until she couldn't stifle her moans. Finally he filled her, moving slowly, deliberately, endlessly. She lost all consciousness of everything but the sensation of being one with him. She gave herself up to being possessed, body and soul. Heat focused and intensified in her belly, her loins, her center, until she thought she couldn't bear another moment. Her body on fire, she arched and crossed the threshold of pleasure so intense it bordered on pain. He swallowed her cry with a kiss that reached into her very soul.

When she recovered conscious awareness she heard him whisper, "I love you, Amalie."

"And I love you, Jonathan." For the moment it didn't matter to her that she was the wrong Amalie.

After that they continued to spend their mornings walking and talking on the beach, and later, fruitlessly working with the museum archives, but Amalie lived for the nights, when she could find exquisite pleasure in his arms.

****

Amalie and Jonathan sat together in the rocking chairs on the veranda and watched the sunrise light the sea. It was a favorite time of day for them both.

They were sitting quietly, hands touching, when Josephina came through the door, uncharacteristically early.

"Good morning, Amalie…Good morning, Jonathan. I trust you both slept well."

Amalie drew in her breath sharply as Jonathan burst out laughing, that deep uninhibited laugh that Amalie had come to love.

"How…?" Amalie was too confused for speech.

"How long have I known Jonathan? For quite some time. I haven't always been able to see him clearly, but I've always known when he was here."

"Can you see him now, Josephina?"

"Not exactly. I know he's here but his outlines are a bit fuzzy. Sometimes I see a sort of aura. I'm an Ansett, too, remember. And sometimes I hear him whistling Greensleeves." She turned to Jonathan. "You always whistle the same phrase. It's enough to drive a body crazy."

Jonathan laughed again. "Sorry. I'll try to remember to do a bit more of it in the future. Or perhaps to whistle another tune."

Josephina nodded. "Thank you." She glanced at Amalie. "Since Amalie's been here I seem to see you and hear you more clearly."

Amalie shook her head. "But why didn't you tell me, Josephina?"

"People already think I'm a little dotty. If I told them I saw ghosts…well, better to keep it to myself."

"It's such a relief to talk to someone else who can see him. I can more than see him, Josephina. To me he is as real as you."

"That's nice."

"But don't you see the dilemma we're facing? Jonathan is a ghost. I'm not."

"I don't see how that's very different from two people of different races or religions falling in love. You're just two people of different times."

"I didn't say anything about love, Josephina."

"You didn't have to. I've watched you together for days now, walking on the beach."

Not having any notion of how to answer that, Amalie changed tactic. "Jonathan has to be here for a reason. He needs to know what happened that night. And I must say we aren't learning much by wading through the museum archives." She shook her head. "And I can't see how my being here can make a difference."

Jonathan answered her. "Your being here makes all the difference in the world. But I think to find out what happened we'll have to go back together, back to eighteen hundred and ten, to the night when everything went wrong. Perhaps to the week or two leading up to that night."

"Oh my." Josephina went quite pale.

Why did that idea not seem crazy to Amalie. "Is it possible to do that?"

Jonathan nodded. "I've done it before. I've gone back and lived those last days over and over, but always the end is the same. I'm carrying you into the house. We've just been secretly wed. I step through the doorway and...nothing. That's the last moment of my life I recall."

"But if it ends that way each time, how can my going back with you help?"

"I think I know the answer to that." Josephina looked at Amalie. "Jonathan is of that moment in history. When Jonathan is there he would have no memory of now. Of his future. But you are of this day and time."

Jonathan nodded. "That's it exactly. There, I have no memory of being a ghost. I have no premonition of what is to come." He turned to Amalie, "But, because your time is of the present, of this time and place, I think it is possible that you will be able to remember the now, to see and understand both as Amalie, my bride, and as my Amalie of this century. You may be able to see and to tell me what happened after I walked through that door. I don't for one moment believe the written accounts."

"But, even assuming I'm willing to do this, how do we get back to the past?"

"When I go I simply cross the threshold of Evans Plantation. There's nothing very exact about it. Sometimes I find myself there two or three weeks before the end, other times I'm there only on the

91

last day. But the crossing has never been difficult." He smiled. "Of course I am, as you would have it, a ghost. I have no idea how or if it will work for you."

"Why do you think taking me back with you will make a difference?"

"You'll be an addition to the equation. Something new. Something that wasn't there before. I think in crossing you will become one with the other Amalie, but I believe you may retain your memory of the present, of this other time and place, as I, a ghost in this time, retain my memory of that other time. Does that make any sense?"

Amalie laughed. "Does any of this make sense? If I stopped to think about it I'd check myself into a loony bin."

"I've been waiting centuries for you to return. Will you help me?"

Amalie looked at Jonathan. He didn't speak again but his eyes pled for understanding, for help.

"I'll try."

Josephina smiled. "Well, I'm glad that's settled. Shall I go pack you a bag? How long will you be gone?"

Jonathan laughed. "It doesn't work that way. We'll return to exactly the day, the same moment, when we left." Then a worried frown crossed his face. "That is if Amalie can return. I'm not sure how that works. I've never tried it with anyone from another age before."

"That's reassuring." Amalie looked at Jonathan and had the fleeting thought that there could be worse things than being stuck with him for eternity. "If we're going to do this, we might as well do it now, before I have time to come to my senses."

His breath came out in a rush. "Thank you."

Amalie kissed Josephina, who wished them good luck and waved them off as if they were going on a school holiday. They took the jeep out to White Wall, where they parked off the road and climbed through the high bush to the old foundations of Evans Plantation house.

"This is it," Jonathan said. "This is where the portal is. When I cross the threshold you must be with me, as close beside me as you can get. I don't know whether it will work. And I don't know exactly where or when we will land. Are you ready to do this?"

Amalie merely nodded.

"Then give me your hands and step with me."

Amalie reached toward him and the faintest brush of an icy breeze touched her fingers. Then the air began to swirl around her and the sky darkened. Wind rushed over and around her. She felt her hands clasped in an iron grip as the earth shook and she tumbled into an abyss, the sound of nothingness roaring in her ears. Consciousness faded.

CHAPTER 5

Everything stilled. She was safe. Amalie was in a spacious bedroom with a canopy bed and beside it a table with an oil lamp. There was a tall mirror. Looking into it, she saw herself, yet not herself. This other Amalie, the one she was now, was younger with hair tumbling down her back in a mass of soft bright curls. Her figure wasn't exactly plump, Amalie thought as she looked critically, but was certainly fuller than her twenty-first century one. And what on earth was she wearing? Pants? She was dressed in boy's clothing? Pants and a loose shirt and boots. Not at all what she expected. She thought nineteenth century ladies always went around in sprigged muslin dresses with multiple petticoats.

She became aware that someone was speaking to her.

"… and you know your Papa would skin me alive if he thought I was lettin' you go out of here dressed like that in the middle of the afternoon when you is supposed to be resting in your room like any other well-bred lady would be."

"Oh, Jemma, don't fuss. He'll never know if you don't tell him. I'll only be gone for a couple of hours. I'll be back well before he has a chance to miss me."

"You goin' out of here dressed in your brother's clothes again. You goin' riding astride like any rag-a-muffin boy. I done tol' your Papa when he let you to ride that way as a chile it were a mistake."

Amalie kissed Jemma's leathery brown wrinkled face. "Don't fuss, Jemma. I hate riding in skirts. And I'll be back before you know it."

She crossed to the door and after checking to make sure no one was around, slipped out and down the back stairs and out the door. She ran to the stables where her mare was waiting, already saddled as she'd instructed. A moment later she was trotting through the fields toward Evans House and Jonathan.

Well, thought Amalie. So I can ride. And I'm no shrinking violet either. Imagine, wearing male clothing in the eighteen hundreds. She settled in, content to let the other her take charge. Odd how she was so conscious of self while her counterpart seemed unaware of the other entity now inhabiting her body.

Amalie cantered along through the cane fields on the rough cart track used when they took cane to the mill at Evans Plantation. The day was hot, the sun burning down on the backs of the field workers engaged in the endless task of weeding rows of cane. They were chanting rhythmically as they worked. They did not pause in their labor to look at her. To do so would have been to earn the wrath of their white driver.

Fifteen minutes later she was at Evans Plantation.

Jonathan turned from where he had been standing by the window as she burst in.

"I just had to see you." Then, seeing the other inhabitant of the room, "Sorry to interrupt your work, Samuel."

The studious looking young black man seated at the desk looked up from his ledgers and peered at her over his glasses. "It's no problem, Miss Amalie. We were almost through here." He turned to Jonathan. "So the answer to your last question is yes, the section we planted in bananas last year has been profitable. It has brought us more revenue for the amount of acreage than the cane." He smiled at Jonathan. "Go on. I'll finish up here."

"Thanks, Samuel. I should be back in a couple of hours."

Without need for words, Jonathan and Amalie climbed hand in hand down the steep cliff path that led to the sea. In moments they were out of sight of the house, alone in a cove shaded by broad leafed sea grape trees, in a world of blue sky, turquoise sea, and black sand.

"You know your father would skin me alive if he knew we were meeting like this."

"I don't see why. After all we've been betrothed for two years." She reached up and kissed him lightly.

"Two of the longest years of my life." Jonathan pulled her into his arms and deepened the kiss. "Much too long. I want to be married to you, Amalie."

She pushed him gently away. "We'll talk later. First we swim. I'm hot from the ride over." As she spoke, Amalie was stripping off her outer clothing. "Race you!" Clad only in her chemise she ran into the sea.

"You're incorrigible," he called after her, shedding his own clothing rapidly and racing after her in the buff.

Amalie stood, the water swirling around her, and watched him. She never tired of looking at his body. He was tall and sinewy, with well-muscled shoulders and arms. His broad chest tapered to a trim waist and below that…a blush rose up her cheeks. He caught up with her when she was waist high in the soft water, getting ready to plunge in. His arms came around her and he kissed her soundly as a breaker crashed over their heads, leaving them both sputtering. Laughing, they swam out to where the water was deep and clear, where the high waves were only gentle rollers. There they floated in contentment. Then, without need for words, they swam in unison for shore and climbed out to throw themselves down on the warm sand. Her chemise, now plastered to her body, revealed more than it concealed.

He reached for her and kissed her again, his tongue caressing hers, his hands moving with the knowledge of familiarity over her full curves. This was no ghostly touch, however. This was flesh and blood meeting flesh and blood. Her nipples, through the wet garment, stiffened under his touch. She felt a throbbing response between her legs. She wanted to cry with the pleasure of it.

His voice was low and rough with passion when he spoke. "You'd better take that thing off. Hang it on a bush to dry."

Amalie shrugged out of the garment. "I'll just leave it with you. No one will see that I'm not wearing anything under my brother's clothing."

Her head was spinning. Yes, she thought. She could feel it all. Feel it as if she were truly the first Amalie. And she desperately wanted this man. Even if it had to be in this way.

Jonathan kissed her deeply again, leaving her breathless. His warm, decidedly human body, covered hers as she brought her arms around him. She slid her hands down to the muscles of his tight buttocks. She recalled that he had once asked her if she could ride. She smiled a secret smile. This might be a good time to show him. She pushed him over so she could rise above him, twisting her hand in the soft curls of his chest hair, kissing him as he so often had kissed her, first teasing his nipples with her tongue then moving down to where she found his throbbing shaft. He moaned and twisted under her ministrations. It was thrilling to have him so alive, so at her mercy, so responsive. To pleasure him as he had pleasured her for the last month. She licked a lazy circle around his erection. He shouted and pulled her up to him, wildly seeking her mouth, his tongue probing as she settled slowly on him, taking him inch by glorious inch into her, wriggling as she did so, enjoying his inarticulate cry. Then she removed herself completely and hovered over him.

"Shall we just take a lazy canter around the park?" she said, taking just the tip of his erection into her, moving her hips in a lazy circle. "Or would milord prefer a gentle trot?" She took a bit more of him into her and moving up and down, only slightly increasing the tempo of her movements. He groaned audibly under her. "Perhaps a gallop?" She moved just a bit faster. Still she had not taken him in fully.

"No" he bellowed, slapping her flanks and turning her over so that she was pinned under him. He was still for a moment. Breathing harshly, hardly able to speak, he said, "It's a race to the finish."

She twisted her head from side to side, trying to escape, not wanting to escape, the mounting tension as he rammed fully into her and rode her wildly until, blind to everything except sensation, in unison they arched and shouted as they came to a tumultuous climax.

He fell on her, drained. When they could again breathe he kissed her, a slow sweet kiss "Wherever did you learn to ride like that, my love?" Then, turning serious, "I love you so much. Why do we have to go on meeting this way? I want to be married to you. Your father long ago gave his approval to our betrothal. I want you in my home, in my bed. Not like this, always stolen moments. Marry me now."

Amalie sighed. "You know why I can't. Mama's in England with my brother until June. You know she and my father want us to wait until she returns."

"I know, my sweet. It just seems so long…"

"I must get back home before I'm missed. Will you be coming for dinner?"

"Your father has invited me. It's torture sitting across the table from you, not able to touch you."

Amalie laughed. "I've been told that self-control builds character." She stood and started pulling on the clothes she had so hastily discarded. "I'll see you this evening." Without waiting for him, Amalie scampered up the cliff, mounted her horse, and was gone.

****

Ansett House was as beautiful by candlelight as Amalie had imagined it when she was in her own century. She moved gracefully through the rooms, her gauzy silk skirts swaying as she walked. She glanced at herself in the great hall mirror as she passed. The tops of her breasts were modestly covered by the lace trimmed neckline of her empire gown. She pulled the bodice down a bit to expose more of the rosy flesh the lace would have hidden. She had a paisley shawl draped over her arms. Her hair was piled high on her head with just a few tendrils cunningly escaping and her tight bodice clearly outlined her figure. This was a far different image than the tomboy she had been only hours ago. She smiled to herself. Jonathan would suffer looking at her across the table tonight.

"Ah there you are, my dear." Her father stood in the doorway to the parlor. "Come and greet our guest."

Amalie wondered briefly why her father should be so formal with respect to Jonathan, but when she entered the room she realized it was not Jonathan she was to greet, but Charles Benstone, the Island Administrator.

"Good evening, Mr. Benstone," she said, trying to keep the dislike out of her voice. "How nice that you could join us."

"Mistress Ansett. You look charming in that frock."

"I'm sure our local fashions must seem quite out of date to one recently from London."

"Not at all."

Amalie studied this man she so unaccountably despised. What was it about him? He cut a handsome figure. All that long dark wavy hair and that almost too perfect face. He was tall and strongly built and dressed in the latest London fashion. He was any woman's dream. Except for something in his expression. There was an arrogance in the way he looked at her, a look of cruelty about his eyes. Amalie had a sense of barely contained brutality in his bearing. She realized he was speaking and she hadn't heard a word he had said. "I'm sorry?"

"I was telling your father that it isn't every evening that I get to dine with such beauty."

"You flatter me, sir." Amalie felt uncomfortable under his scrutiny. Why had her father invited this odious man to join them for dinner?

Jonathan arrived at that moment, hurrying into the room, apologizing. "Sorry I'm late. Had a lame horse to attend to..." He stopped short on seeing the Administrator.

"Benstone." He bowed stiffly.

"Good evening, Mr. Evans. I wasn't aware that we were to be dinner companions."

"Nor was I."

Benstone turned to Emile Ansett. "Perhaps I should explain. Mr. Evans and I had a minor altercation last week at the slave auction. We were bidding on the same pretty piece of flesh. He outbid me, I'm afraid. And I'm unaccustomed to losing."

"She had a young child you were unwilling to take with her."

"Don't believe in keeping slave families together. Spoils them for work. Better if all family ties are severed."

"I know that's the popular opinion. I don't happen to hold with it."

"So it would seem. So it seems she will warm your bed rather than mine. A pity."

Amalie bit back the sharp retort she felt rising. Jonathan would never bed a slave. Nor any unwilling woman.

Jonathan glanced at Amalie. "Do not judge others by your own behaviors, Benstone. And remember that there is a lady present."

"Apologies, Mistress Amalie." He bowed and smiled a mirthless smile, then turned back to Jonathan. "I've heard that you have some outlandish notions about freeing the slaves. It seems to me, Mr. Evans, that you don't fully understand how important slavery is to the economy of this small island. The sugar cane trade would perish without it."

"I believe that sugar is the curse of the Caribbean. It has brought economic, social, and political upheaval to these islands. It cannot be profitable without slave labor, and, with all due respect, Mr. Benstone, the days of slavery are numbered. The trade is already illegal."

"The actions of a misguided government. What has been enacted can always be repealed."

Emile Ansett intervened. "I believe dinner is ready. Gentlemen, Amalie." Taking his daughter's arm, he led the small group into the dining room.

When dinner, an interminable affair, was finally over Amalie's father indicated that he wished to meet with the Administrator alone. He spoke to Jonathan. "Perhaps you and Amalie would like to take a turn in the garden. We shan't be long."

"Certainly, sir."

Once out of hearing of the house, Amalie sputtered out her rage. "That horrible man. I don't for one moment believe what he implied. But I'm afraid you have made an enemy there, Jonathan."

Jonathan shrugged. "I find myself increasingly at odds with the whole notion of slavery. I've been reading a new treatise by a man named Wilberforce in England. He considers slavery to be an act against the will of God. I tend to agree with him. It's degrading to both owners and victims."

"But how would you ever be able to run Evans Plantation without slaves?"

"There are alternatives. I'm not convinced that it would cost much more to hire help than it does to buy people then house and clothe and feed them. And I'm experimenting with other crops, bananas, lemons, and tobacco. None of those are as labor intensive as cane. He frowned. I hate cane. It's a brutalizing crop."

He looked at Amalie and smiled. "But this isn't a conversation for tonight. You look so lovely. I could hardly take my eyes off you long enough to eat." He pulled her to him and sent soft feathery kisses over her lips, her neck, her breasts, then back to her lips where he lingered.

Amalie was weak with desire. She leaned into his tall frame, ran her hands down his body, pausing where she found the evidence of his arousal.

He groaned. "Don't. I can't control myself if you do that and if your father and Benstone should come out of the study..."

"Mmm. I rather think I should like to see you lose control. But you're right. We'd best pull ourselves together and get back to the house. Shall I come tomorrow afternoon? We could just meet at the beach. That way your household won't be aware."

"The beach would be best. But it's not my household I'm worried about. It's yours. If we go on this way we're very likely to get caught. I'm not concerned for myself, but your reputation…"

"Oh, bullocks! We are surely not the first betrothed couple to bed before the wedding. But I shall take care that no one sees me. Until tomorrow, then." Amalie reached up and planted a tantalizing kiss on his lips, then turned back toward the house.

****

The next days passed in a haze of joy. They met at the beach every day, their hunger for each other unending. Amalie found that she was more and more deeply involved emotionally with Jonathan. It wasn't just the sex, although she admitted to herself that the sex was fantastic, it was his innate goodness, his sense of honor. He was unlike any man she'd ever known. She knew she was deeply in love with him. In love with a man who died two hundred years ago who was in love with another Amalie from another time.

The only shadow on their days was the increasing presence of Benstone at Ansett House. He seemed to be there almost every evening and Jonathan, who had always previously been invited to their evening meal, was now more and more excluded. When Amalie asked her father why, he was evasive.

It was a month later that events took a sharp turn. Amalie was very late coming to the beach. She found Jonathan distraught when she arrived.

"I didn't know whether something had gone wrong. I was deeply worried. Your father has been so cool to me lately. I'm hardly ever invited to Ansett House any more. And Benstone always seems to be there." He held her tight to him and buried his face in her hair. "I cannot lose you. I cannot live without you."

"Oh, my darling, I'm so sorry I was late. Father wanted to see me. I'm not sure what about. He hemmed and hawed and in the end just kissed me on the cheek and sent me on my way. It's so unlike him. Something's up and I don't know what. I can only stay a short while."

"We can't go on this way. I have this terrible feeling that something's wrong. Almost like an evil presence hovering nearby. Marry me, Amalie. Marry me now."

"I've told you why that's not possible." She paused and looked at him mischievously. "Of course, if I were to find myself with child…"

"You're not!" Jonathan looked into her eyes searchingly then cupped her face gently in his hands. "We must marry immediately. There can be no further delay."

"I'm not sure. It's been only a month. Perhaps we should wait another week or two…"

"I think it would be better to elope now and present your family with a fait acompli."

"I don't think that will be necessary. If we tell my father the circumstances, I'm sure he'll agree to our immediate marriage. I'd hate to marry without his knowledge."

"A child," he mused. "Nothing could make me happier. I'll speak to your father tomorrow."

"I'd best be getting back." Amalie made a wry face. "Mr. Benstone is coming to dinner again. It won't be an easy evening. I really can't abide the man. I can't imagine why Papa invites him so often."

"Well, as Administrator of St. Clement's, Benstone's in a position of some considerable influence. Perhaps your father has business dealings with him."

"I don't know. They're closeted in Papa's office for hours at a time. And when he finally leaves, Papa seems, I don't know, somehow worried, distracted. And he either snaps at me if I ask him about it or he tells me not to worry my pretty little head. I hate being treated as if I'm brainless."

Jonathan laughed. "You're far from brainless. Willful, impetuous, even capricious at times, but never brainless."

He became serious. "I love you, Amalie. I love you to the depths of my being. I have always loved you. I shall always love you. I shall love you in this life and in the next, through eternity. You hold my soul in your hands."

Amalie looked into his eyes and saw fear, a bleakness there that terrified her. She held him tight to her. "And I love you, Jonathan." She pulled away reluctantly. "I must go home, before I'm missed."

An hour later, Jemma was brushing out her hair and muttering. "Hair full of sand and salt water again. We got it wash all out but it still damp...Not gonna be dry in time for dinner. We just gonna have to fasten it up and hope your papa don't notice."

"It will be fine, Jemma. Just help me with lacing up these stays."

Jemma took the whalebone garment, placed it around Amalie's slim waist and started pulling on the laces. She chuckled. "You gainin' weight. Better start thinkin' about what you eats. Mr. Jonathan maybe not gonna want a fat wife. "

Amalie grunted as Jemma pulled the laces tighter. "I hate stays. When I'm married I'm never going to wear stays again. I hear that in England and France now they're wearing soft loose gowns with almost nothing under them."

Jemma huffed. "You not gonna be wearing no gowns with nothin' under them while I draws breath."

Amalie's response was muffled as Jemma put her lacy petticoat over her head, pulled it into place, and started hooking it up the back. This was followed by a high waisted, full skirted, peach silk dress with a low neckline and short full sleeves edged in lace.

After Jemma buttoned the twenty small silk covered buttons down the back, she stood back to admire her handiwork. "You'll do. Now get downstairs. You is late."

When Amalie entered the drawing room she found only Mr. Benstone there. She nodded her greeting and walked past him out to the terrace.

He followed her. "Your father has very kindly allowed me this time alone with you in which to speak."

"To speak? To speak about what?"

He raised one eyebrow and his lips curved in a sardonic smile. "Surely you know about what. I've been a regular guest here of late. It cannot have escaped your attention that for some time my interest in you has been more than casual and your father has encouraged that interest."

"Encouraged?" Amalie's mind was whirling. What was he talking about?

He crossed the room and took her hands in his. She tried to free them, but found them locked in an iron grip.

"I have the honor to ask you to be my wife. To share my life, my place in the Governor's Mansion." He leaned forward and kissed her even as she tried to twist away. He put his hands firmly on her shoulders and warned, "Don't pull away from me. Don't ever try to resist when I'm kissing you. You won't like the result." He brought his mouth down to hers again. His kiss was fierce. It smacked not of love but of conquest.

Amalie tore away from him and ran into the parlor as her father entered. With her father behind her for support, she turned back toward the man who had just assaulted her.

"I'm sorry you've come to an erroneous conclusion, Mr. Benstone, but surely my father must have informed you that I am betrothed to another."

He father's voice was low and reluctant. "We can hardly be bound by an informal arrangement made when you were little more than a child, Amalie."

Amalie turned to her father in astonishment. "What are you saying, Papa? You gave your word to Jonathan. We love each other. We plan to be married soon."

Her father avoided looking at her. "Plans change. And love is often a poor basis for a marriage. Mr. Benstone can give you rank and position. He's not some struggling planter, he's financially secure. I've promised your hand to Mr. Benstone and that's that. To fit in with Mr. Benstone's planned trip to London, the wedding will take place just after Christmas. Your mother will be sorry to miss it, but she'll understand."

"No!" Amalie looked at her father in disbelief. He looked away from her. She whirled around and ran out of the room. Upstairs, she threw herself down on her bed in a storm of tears. How could her father do this to her?

Jemma opened the door. In a moment Amalie was in the older woman's arms, sobbing against her cushiony breast.

"What's wrong, chile?"

"It's Papa. He wants me to marry that odious Benstone. Why, Jemma? I don't understand."

"You just has to talk with him. Your papa, he's a good man. He won't be forcin' you to marry one man when you loves another."

"But he says he will."

"Tomorrow you talk to him. He'll change his mind when he see how you feelin' about it." Jemma tucked her in as she used to when Amalie was a child. "Get some rest now."

When Amalie heard Benstone's carriage leaving she dried her tears and ventured downstairs. She would try to talk to her father now. Quietly, rationally. Surely he could be made to change his mind.

She went into his study and was shocked to see him sitting at his desk, his shoulders slumped, his head in his hands.

111

"Papa what is it? Why are you doing this to me? You don't want to."

He turned and hugged her. "No, my child. I don't want to. But if I don't, we're ruined. We could lose everything."

"But how?"

"It was a business arrangement. The plantation has been losing money for the last several years. The cost of running it keeps going up and the price of sugar keeps going down."

"I had no idea. You never said anything. You sent my brother to that expensive English boarding school. And when Mama wanted to take that costly trip to London you said nothing. How could the plantation be losing money?"

"The European market for sugar has almost completely disappeared. First, the wars made the shipping by sea dangerous then the discovery by the Europeans that they could produce sugar from beets finished us. We have a plantation to support. Several hundred mouths to feed. I was desperate. What was I to do?"

Amalie felt a chill down her spine. "What *did* you do?"

"I went into business with Benstone. When Parliament abolished the slave trade two years ago, the price of slaves doubled then doubled again. The Americans and the Spanish are clamoring for more slaves and the British boats that supplied them are no longer allowed to serve their needs. At least not legitimately. But, illegally, that's another matter. There are vast profits to be made for minimal investment for those willing to engage in the illicit trade, smuggling slaves."

"Oh, Papa, you didn't."

"I did. And for a while everything was fine. I was able to pay our bills and keep this place going. I could buy you pretty frocks and send Tommy off to school in England."

"What went wrong?"

"When I got enough money ahead, I told Benstone I wanted out of the arrangement. That I no longer wanted any part in the trade." Her father paused. "That's when he told me. The only name on any of the ownership papers is mine. And he holds the papers."

"I don't understand."

"What I did is against the law, Amalie. If Benstone speaks to the right people, I could go to jail for years. This house, this property, could be confiscated."

"But you said Benstone brought you into this. He was a partner in it."

"There is no evidence of that. He says it's my name, and my name only, on the documents."

"But I still don't understand what that has to do with me and my marriage to Jonathan."

"For some reason Benstone has decided that you would make, as he put it, the perfect wife for a man aspiring to be Governor of the

British Islands. And he pointed out to me in no uncertain terms that as his father-in-law, I should, of course, have nothing to fear."

"Oh, Papa. I'm so sorry. But I can't marry Mr. Benstone, not even to save Ansett House, not even to keep you out of jail. I think I'm with child."

"You're what?"

Amalie heard rage and frustration in her father's voice.

"I'm carrying Jonathan's child. We were going to tell you tomorrow. We must be married quickly and quietly and we want your blessing."

"You will be married quickly and quietly married, my girl, but not to Jonathan Evans. You will indeed marry Benstone. But this changes everything. I have to get to work on this. I must get word to your future husband that you have agreed to the wedding and wish it to take place immediately. And you will not tell him of your…indiscretion. Time is of the essence. He must be made to believe that the child is his. Now go to your room."

Amalie looked at her father in disbelief, then turned and walked slowly out of the room and upstairs.

She put on the boy's clothing she'd discarded in the afternoon after her meeting with Jonathan. Thank goodness Jemma hadn't yet taken them to wash.

She opened the door a crack and seeing no one in the hall, made her way quickly down the back stairs, out of the house, and to the stable. She opened the door, alert to the squeal it sometimes made and stepped softly so as not to awaken the stable hands. Her mare greeted her with a whinny, surprised to see her at this time of night. Amalie quieted her with a stroke and a murmur. She quickly saddled her and moved outside into the black of the night. Once mounted, she kept a slow cautious pace until they were out of hearing. Then she leaned forward, gave her mount a nudge and inveigled, "Go, Molly!"

The horse took off like a bolt of lightning. Moments later they were at Evans House. Tying her horse loosely to the post outside the front door, she bounded up the steps and through the door. She found him working in his office.

Jonathan took one look at her tear stained face, her disheveled hair, and was up instantly, his arms around her. Now that she was here, safe in his arms she began to sob uncontrollably. He held her until she quieted.

"What is it, love? Nothing can be all that bad." He took her over to the settee and gently wiped away her tears. "Tell me."

She did, in all its detail. Once she started, the whole story spilled out, words tumbling over words.

Jonathan sat in silence until she had finished. Then he said, "There are two separate problems here. The first is our marriage and our coming child. Nothing is more important than that. The second is how to save your father from the potential disaster he has brought down on himself and his household. I believe I may have some ideas as to how we can resolve that, but that will come after."

"After?"

"After we are safely married."

"And how are we to accomplish that, without my father's consent?"

"People do elope. Right after you told me you might be with child, I spoke with Brother Xavier. I thought time might be of the essence. I told him frankly of our situation. He has made all the arrangements for our immediate marriage, foregoing the usual formalities."

"How ever did he get the parish priest to agree to something like that?"

"The church needs a new roof. So, my dear, are you ready to come to St. Agatha's with me?"

"Now? Tonight?"

"I think we must do this immediately. I suspect nothing can be gained by further discussion."

Amalie looked down at her brother's wrinkled pants. "This isn't exactly the wedding dress I had imagined."

"No matter. You can have a dozen wedding dresses later if you wish."

It was after midnight when, accompanied by Brother Xavier and Samuel, they roused Father Martin from his slumbers. At first the priest demurred, telling them to come back in the morning. When Jonathan insisted and mentioned a new marble baptismal font to go with the anticipated new roof, the priest relented. If he thought the bride's wedding attire a little unorthodox, he was too discrete to mention it. Brother Xavier and Samuel served as witnesses. The priest was a bit taken aback at having a Negro as a witness, but gave in as there was clearly no one else available.

Once back at the plantation house, Jonathan scooped Amalie up into his arms and stepped across the threshold. "Welcome to your new home, my love." He stumbled, a look of shock on his face. Slowly he crumpled.

Amalie fell to the floor then scrambled up. That was when she saw the knife sticking out of her husband's back and blood trickling between his lips. She started to scream, her voice a high piercing wail.

"For God's sake will somebody shut that woman up?" Charles Benstone stepped out of the shadows.

"You weren't supposed to kill him." Amalie's father stood on the landing. "You were just supposed to rescue my daughter."

"Don't be a fool. Did you think he wouldn't have come after me?"

117

Emile Ansett shook his head. "This was no part of our plan. I can't countenance murder."

"You won't have to." Benstone nodded to his assistant. "Smithins?"

The huge man who doubled as valet and assassin to the Administrator stepped forward and shot Amalie's father through the heart. He was dead before his body hit the floor.

Amalie could hear a distant voice screaming and screaming as she felt herself falling into darkness.

Turning to the man at his elbow, Benstone said, "Wrap her up and take her to my carriage. And make her stop that caterwauling."

As suddenly as the unearthly screaming had begun, it ceased.

"Good. She's stopped that infernal racket."

But Amalie had not stopped screaming. Others could no longer hear it, but in her head the screaming continued, driving out all thought, all memory, all sanity. She could hear distant voices, but the words made no sense to her.

That other Amalie, the one who didn't belong here, knew she had to find her way out or go insane with her ancestor. She plunged and separated herself from the silently screaming woman and made her way to the threshold, unseen and unfelt. But she needed to know what was to happen next. She turned toward the voices.

The assassin was a huge man, perhaps six foot five. His swarthy face was pockmarked and his hands were the size of hams. He was speaking.

"What about these bodies? There's bound to be questions."

"You already have Evan's nigger, Samuel. We'll put him in jail. We'll blame the murders on him. Who's going to question the word of a slave against that of the Island Administrator?" Benstone gave a sly smile. "Better still, we can have him shot while trying to escape. Any evidence will unfortunately be lost in the fire Samuel set before his capture."

He nodded toward the figure of Amalie, unseeing, locked away in some distant place. "Take her back to the Governor's Mansion. The preacher is waiting and the wedding will take place tonight. I'm not taking any further chances. I've been patient too long as it is. She'll keep quiet. I'll see to it that she doesn't speak to anyone about what happened here. Not unless she wants the rest of her family to join her father."

As they left, flames shot up and shouts and cries could be heard from the slave quarters.

Amalie was unaware of being bundled up in a blanket and carried not very gently in strong arms to the waiting coach. The other Amalie was a silent observer and an unseen passenger.

Later that night, Amalie watched as her mirror image, unable to stand without being supported, was married to Charles Benstone. To

119

the minister's request that she repeat her vows, she gave no response, but this did not deter him from duly pronouncing the couple husband and wife.

Amalie was an unwilling witness as the marriage was consummated within the hour. She had no desire to be there, but she was held by her pity for the girl and the hope that she might be able somehow to intervene. She was powerless to help, but could see the bride was completely untouched by what was happening. Her mind had withdrawn to safety in some far distant place.

As Amalie turned to leave this scene of tragedy, she heard Benstone muttering, "Might as well be fucking a corpse."

Dazed, she wandered the long road back to Evans Plantation, where she only hoped there would be a portal to her world.

It was almost dawn when she arrived back at the now smoldering ruins of Evans House, weary and despondent. What would she do if she couldn't find a way back to her own time, her own world? She sat down by the side of the road, leaning against the trunk of a knip tree, pulled her legs up and wrapped her arms around them. Her head drooped. She was so tired.

CHAPTER 6

She must have slept, although she didn't know how she could have when she was in such a perilous situation. But it was now daylight and the sun was shining brightly. She lifted her head and looked around her.

The jeep was there. It was sitting in front of her, right where she had parked it, when? Three weeks ago, a month ago? No. Jonathan had told her they would return to the same day, the same moment. She glanced at her watch. Yes. Her watch was on her wrist once again and it was working. It was one o'clock. Exactly when they had crossed the portal.

Stiffly, Amalie got up and walked over to the jeep. A short time later she was back at the beach house. Josephina was having a late lunch on the veranda.

"Come and join me, my dear. Elvirna has made lobster salad and it's delicious."

Amalie realized with a start that she was, indeed, hungry. She sat at the place set for her.

"When will you and Jonathan try to go into the past?" Josephina queried. " I thought you were going today."

There was a catch in Amalie's voice as she said, "We did go today. We were there in the past for more than a month, but when I came back it was still today. Oh, Josephina, I can't bear it. How can I tell him what happened? And I haven't even seen him yet. What if he wasn't able to come back?"

"He'll come back, my dear, of course he will. He always has. What did you learn?"

"Benstone murdered Jonathan in cold blood. He killed my father, too. And set up Samuel to take the blame. He planned to have Samuel shot while trying to escape." Amalie put her head in her hands and tears trickled through her fingers. At this highly charged moment, under intense emotional stress, she was unaware that she was still thinking of Emile Ansett as her father.

Josephina stood and went over to Amalie, putting her arms around her and patting her back.

"There, darling. You were very brave. It has been a stressful time for you." She gently led the unresisting Amalie indoors and up to her bedroom. There she helped her undress and settled her into the bed, pulling the light coverlet over her.

"Get some rest, dear. We'll talk later."

In her room, Amalie replayed the events of her experience in another time, in another woman's body. The horror of those last hours was there, bloody and terrifying. But so was the memory of what happened before that, many times, on the beach. Her body vibrated with the memory of his hands on her, his kisses, the way he felt inside her. She gave a small laugh of self-derision. She was in love with a ghost. With a man two hundred odd years old. A man she couldn't properly love back, hold, caress in her own time. Oh, he could give her sexual satisfaction, even in his ghostly form. He did, often. But she could not properly reciprocate. How crazy was that?

Yet she desperately wanted to see him again. Even if she couldn't embrace him in the way she had in the nineteenth century. Just to see his beloved face, to sit and talk with him. Why had he not come back? Of course, they had been spectacularly unsuccessful in changing anything. Perhaps he had just given up. If so she hoped he would truly rest in peace. The thought gave her unutterable pain.

For the next two days she walked the beach, hoping against hope that he would appear to her, but with each passing hour, hope faded.

On the third day after her return, Lorna called again.

"Lorna! I've been meaning to call. How are you? How are things going with the business?"

"Just fine, no thanks to your input." Lorna laughed, taking the sting out of the words.

"What's the weather like in L.A.? The usual November chill and rain?"Amalie asked.

"I wouldn't know. From where I'm standing it's sunny and downright hot."Lorna answered.

Puzzled, Amalie said, "Where are you?"

123

"I'm in what passes for an airport on this tiny rock that has held your attention for the last few weeks. I've come to see what's going on."

"You're here?" Amalie's voice rose, "You're on St. Clement's?"

"I am. And you'd better come and get me before I melt. It's hotter than Hades here. How do you stand it?"

"It's only hot in the middle of the island where the airport is. After all, this is the tropics. "Here on the sea there's always a breeze. I'll be there in ten minutes."

Amalie went out to the veranda where Josephina was sitting in her rocking chair, reading.

"My business partner has just arrived. She's at the airport now. Do we have room for her here? I suppose we could bunk together, but it would be a little snug. Lorna's not a small woman."

"How nice for you. Of course we have room. I'll just have Elvirna make up the back room on the first floor. There's a good double bed in there and it has a pleasant view over the garden. I'll have to find someplace to store all the suitcases and other miscellaneous bits and pieces that have found their way there in recent years. I'll get Elvirna's son, Johnny, to help. I'm sure we can have it ready in a jiffy."

"If you're sure it's not too much trouble."

"Not at all. I've been meaning to do something about that room for months. Now it will happen."

"Thanks, Josephina," she called over her shoulder as she rushed out the door to the jeep.

She came to a screeching halt in front of the tiny terminal building, jumped out, and rushed inside. Lorna was standing beside a pile of Louis Vuitton luggage, looking wilted and very out of place in her west coast business suit.

The two women hugged. "Oh, Lorna. Why didn't you tell me you were coming? I'd have been here when the plane came in." Amalie grabbed the two smaller bags and Lorna followed, wheeling her larger one out to the curb.

"I didn't know if I'd be able to break free. It was a last minute thing."

"It's wonderful to have you here."

Lorna settled back in her seat. "I had to come see what was keeping you here. You're positively glowing. I'd never have thought your skin would take the sun so well. You're all rosy and your hair has turned an even paler more beautiful shade, if that were possible." She looked searchingly at Amalie. "But it's more than that. There's a man, isn't there?"

"Don't be ridiculous, Lorna. I spend my mornings in a musty museum, my afternoons on the beach, and my evenings playing cribbage with Josephina."

"Well, something has given you that glow. And I don't believe for a minute that it's all from the sun."

125

Amalie clamped her mouth shut, thinking, of course there's a man. And if you knew I was in love with a ghost, what would you say then?

She drove through the gate and pulled up in front of the house.

"This is lovely. But it isn't at all the way I imagined a house in the Caribbean. It's so sort of staid and British."

"It's more than a hundred years old and this is a British island."

They found Josephina in the back room, arranging a bowl of frangipani on the night stand. The bed was freshly made with crisp white embroidered linens and the casement windows were open to the garden, letting in the refreshing breeze. The old suitcases and other assorted debris that had cluttered the room had disappeared.

"You must be Josephina. Thank you for having me. Especially on such short notice."

"It's no bother at all. I'm delighted to meet Amalie's friend and partner. I hope you'll enjoy your stay here. I'll leave you to get settled in."

Amalie sat on the bed as Lorna unpacked.

"So tell me," Lorna said as she slipped her frothy underwear into a drawer and then shook out the soft, bright colored silk shirts she loved to wear. "What's keeping you here if it's not a man?"

Amalie was quiet for a moment. There was no way she could confide in Lorna. Not about this. She was in love with a man who died two hundred years ago. How could she tell Lorna that? But she had a feeling that she might have stayed on this island even if she'd never met Jonathan. Even if she hadn't loved Jonathan.

"It's hard to explain," she began. "This place just creeps under your skin. I love it. With the goats and cows holding up traffic, and the electrical outages, and the water that stops flowing when I have my hair full of shampoo."

"That all sounds positively delightful."

"With the warm Caribbean Sea at my door and the unbelievable sunsets and the pet rooster who eats crumbs out of my hand. And Josephina. She's a perpetual delight. I don't know exactly what it is, but I feel at home here. I shall hate to leave."

Lorna looked at her intently. "You really mean that, don't you?"

"Yes. Yes, I do."

"Well, we have a week to talk about it. You must show me your island."

And Amalie did. All thoughts of Jonathan were pushed aside. Amalie took Lorna, as Josephina had taken her, all over the island. She introduced her to the people she had met. She took her everyplace but out on White Wall. She couldn't quite face returning there, not yet. On their fifth day together, Lorna asked about the museum.

"It's interesting. A slice of how life was in those early years."

"You said there was a portrait there?"

Amalie realized that she wanted to show Lorna. To see what her reaction might be. "We can go this morning." Amalie's stomach churned. She'd not set foot in the museum since the last time she was there with Jonathan.

Gustavia greeted them as they entered.

"This is my friend and business partner from California, Lorna Cummings. Lorna, Gustavia Graham. Her family has been on the island forever."

"I'm enjoying visiting your island."

"I'm glad. Are you here to help Amalie with the archives?"

Lorna glanced in confusion at Amalie, who hastened to say, "No. Lorna's here on a short holiday. I know I've been neglecting the work here, but I'll get back to it next week. We're just here to see the museum today."

"Please, go on in."

They wandered through the rooms, Amalie avoiding the parlor much as her cousin had, until Lorna said, "All right. Where is it?"

"Just through here."

Lorna walked in and stood wordlessly in front of the portrait. Finally she shook her head and said, "It's uncanny. I've seen family resemblance before, but this is unreal."

Amalie smiled, thinking, you don't know the half of it.

Her partner then moved to the next portrait, the one of Benstone. "This was her husband? Poor girl. She must have had a difficult time of it. I've never seen a meaner looking bastard. Let's get out of here. These portraits give me the creeps."

When they arrived back at the beach house there was an ambulance in front of it and Elvirna was standing in the doorway wringing her hands.

The doors to the ambulance closed with a bang and the vehicle screeched out of the drive spraying gravel. The siren sounded as it made its way up the road toward the hospital.

Panicked, Amalie rushed up the steps and into the house. "Josephina!"

"She not here," Elvirna sobbed. "They done take her to hospital."

"What happened?"

"I don't know. One minute she standin' in the kitchen talkin' about what she want for dinner, the next she on the floor, out cold."

Amalie turned and ran back to the jeep.

"Wait! I'm coming, too." The car was already rolling as Lorna jumped in.

At the small hospital, they paced until the doctor came to join them. "You can go in now. She's drowsy but for the moment she's stable."

"What happened?"

"She has a heart condition. Didn't she tell you?"

"No. She never said a word."

"When she does too much, this happens, After all, she's eighty-five."

"Will she be all right?"

"I think so. We'll keep her for a couple of days to be sure, but when we release her she's got to take it easy."

"I'll see to that, doctor. Thank you."

Later, over dinner, Lorna said, "I guess you won't be coming back with me, will you?"

"Oh, Lorna, how can I? Elvirna would do anything for Josephina, but she's not young and what's more Josephina won't listen to her. She just says 'Oh don't fuss'. I've heard her say that a dozen times. I didn't understand why until this happened. Josephina needs me. I can't leave now."

"I've suspected ever since I arrived that you might not be coming back any time soon." Lorna hesitated. "I have an idea. What you've always contributed to the business, what you supply that I can't, is your imagination, your artistic ability. You always see unique design possibilities, ways of advertising cleverly. I'm good at the business end. At finding the clients and getting the accounts. That's what has made our partnership work so well."

Amalie smiled. "Maybe. I always figured it was the fact that we're really good friends."

"That, too. But there's no getting away from the fact that without your input we wouldn't have gotten where we are."

"And without your ability to close deals, to bring in clients, there wouldn't have been any Ansett-Cummings."

"That's my point. To make the business work we each need what the other has to offer. I have to be in L.A. to do what I do, but there's no reason you can't do what you do, the design work, from here."

"Do you think so?' Amalie felt as if a weight had been lifted from her shoulders. "Yes, of course I could. I could work at it while I'm looking after Josephina. Oh, thank you Lorna. That's a wonderful solution for the moment." Amalie paused. "But if we do this, I want the salary for the student helper you've hired to come out of my earnings. After all you wouldn't need her if I were there."

"Fair enough. Agreed."

The last two days of Lorna's holiday were spent running back and forth to the hospital, with only occasional moments taken out for a short swim or a stroll on the beach.

"I can see why you love this place," Lorna commented on the night before she left as they lingered over after dinner drinks on the veranda. "It suits you." She laughed. "But after a week here I'm longing for city lights. Too quiet here for me."

Josephina came home the day after Lorna left. She moved into the ground floor room Lorna had just vacated, the doctor having

131

prohibited steps. There she was hopelessly pampered by both Elvirna and Amalie until she rebelled and threatened to move out unless they gave her some space.

"She back to she self," Elvirna complained to Amalie. "No holdin' she down."

Amalie hadn't returned to the museum. She didn't want to leave Josephina alone for that long. Instead, she spent her mornings working on her laptop on the new accounts Lorna had sent her. But on the day Josephina so vociferously asserted her independence, she decided perhaps she could safely take a little time in the afternoon for a swim.

The water was warm and embracing. For the first time in days Amalie relaxed. The tension of which she had been almost unaware slipped away as she floated effortlessly on the gentle waves. Her mind turned to the afternoons she'd spent swimming with Jonathan in that other time and place then without her willing it, to their love making on the beach. Would there ever again be anything like that for her? Her body tingled with remembered caresses. She recalled his hands tracing her breasts, her stomach, her thighs. She could almost feel him inside her. She wanted Jonathan Evans. It wasn't just the sex, although God knows that was incredible. She loved him. She admitted to herself that however impossible it seemed, she loved him. She loved Jonathan Evans with a passion that made her marriage to Brett seem silly and shallow by comparison. Even at the beginning, Brett had never touched the chords of response from her that Jonathan could bring by a look, by his merest touch.

She would probably never see him again. Was she sorry she stepped through the portal with him? No, she decided. A love like that was worth any suffering that followed. Just to have experienced it once was a gift.

A tune drifted on the air. Someone was whistling. It couldn't be. Swiftly she started swimming toward the beach. When she splashed ashore no one was there. Had it been her overactive imagination, just wishful thinking?

Her shoulders slumped as she walked back to the house.

Josephina was on the veranda when she climbed the steps from the beach. "Go shower and change. Elvirna has our supper almost ready and I'm looking forward to a sunset drink and then beating you at cribbage tonight."

Amalie laughed. "Yes, ma'am." She saluted and went quickly upstairs, her heart lighter. She loved Josephina. So different from her mother and yet family. After her mother's death, Amalie had resigned herself to being without family. How fortunate she was to have found this cousin, this delightful old lady.

Early the next morning when Amalie took her coffee out to the veranda he was there, rocking and whistling softly to himself.

Amalie nearly dropped her cup. She burst into tears. "I thought you were gone. I thought I'd never see you again."

"I've been here. It seemed wiser not to show myself to you whilst your friend was here. And then you were nursing Josephina. It seemed better to remain unseen. I'm sorry if I've caused you distress."

Amalie fought for control. "I've missed you. Oh Jonathan, what are we to do?

"I don't know. Let's walk on the beach. We have much to talk about and it won't do for Elvirna to come out here and find you talking to yourself again."

Amalie followed Jonathan down the stone steps to the beach and they walked along at the edge of the surf until they were some distance from the house. There they stopped and he turned to her. "You were there. What happened?"

Amalie closed her eyes remembering the pain and confusion of that dreadful night. "They were waiting for you at the house. My father, Amalie's father, that is. He must have checked my room and found me gone. He went to Benstone for help. Benstone brought that man of his, Smithins. He's a killer. They were waiting for us. You were stabbed to death and my father was shot."

"Oh God! It's worse than I feared. But Amalie, what happened to Amalie? You were as one with her. What happened?"

Amalie shuddered. "She started screaming and couldn't stop. Then she became deathly still. I think she was in shock. I separated from her. They couldn't see me but I could see and hear everything."

"And then?"

"Her mind…I don't know, it just seemed to snap. She lost all awareness of her surroundings. She retreated from reality. She was alive, but she wasn't, if that makes any sense to you."

Jonathan stifled a sob.

"They took her to the Governor's Mansion and Benstone married her that night. I was there. She made no response during the ceremony, but the preacher declared them married anyway. If it's any consolation, she never knew what was happening, not then, not later. She was safe in some distant place. Only the shell of what had been Amalie was there."

"My poor darling. She was so young, so unprepared for that."

They trudged on in silence for a few minutes. Then Jonathan, his voice full of anguish, cried, "Why am I still walking between this world and the next? Why am I not with her?"

"I don't know, Jonathan. I wish I could help you, but I don't know." Amalie had tears in her eyes.

"Oh, my sweet Amalie." He brushed his hand across her face and she felt the faintest stir of air. "You help me just by being here. In two hundred years, you are the only person with whom I've been

135

able to talk, to say more than a few words. The first person to see me as more than a phantom, a ghost. Something to be frightened of."

"I could never fear you, Jonathan. I love you."

"And I love you. You are my Amalie, both in this century and in my own. I hate being alive yet not alive, dead yet not dead."

They stood in silence not knowing what more to say, what more to do. Finally Jonathan said, "You'd best be getting back. They'll miss you." He kissed her softly then turned and strode down the beach. Amalie watched as his figure became mist and disappeared.

She sighed and walked slowly back to the house, her head down, her eyes blurred by tears.

When she reached the veranda she was surprised to see Josephina staring down at the beach where she had been only moments earlier with Jonathan.

"He's back. You've been talking with Jonathan Evans," Josephina stated matter-of-factly.

"Yes, he's back." Amalie smiled. She could not keep the joy out of her voice. "Jonathan's back."

"I'm so glad, my dear. But whatever it was that the two of you were talking about, it upset you. What was it?"

At that moment Elvirna pushed through the door with their breakfast. "Got fresh papaya this mornin' and garden omelets with scones to follow. Got to get your energy back up." She pushed

Josephina gently into her chair. "Don't remember sayin' you could have your breakfast out here. I was set to bring it to your room."

"I'm tired of being cooped up, treated like an invalid. Surely it can do no harm to have my breakfast out here where I can breathe in the fresh air and see the sea."

"Maybe not. But the doctor say…"

"Oh, blast the doctor. He's a boy of forty. What does he know?"

Amalie laughed and Elvirna smiled in spite of herself. And as usual, Josephina got her own way.

CHAPTER 7

Jonathan didn't come to her that night or the next and Amalie had difficulty sleeping. She found her thoughts returning to what Josephina had said before their journey to the past. Was it conceivable? Was it possible for the past to be changed? Could they alter history? Prevent Jonathan's murder? Her mind raced ahead. If they could, perhaps Jonathan and Amalie, that other Amalie, could live out their lives in peace, have children, grow old together.

But if that night could be erased then what about her? Where would that leave her? She would have nothing, not even the ghost of Jonathan to give her solace. Jonathan in that past time might have years of contentment with his beloved Amalie, but she, today's Amalie, would lose the only man she had ever loved. How could she bear that?

Bleary eyed from lack of sleep, Amalie waited on the veranda for Jonathan. Once again he didn't come.

At nine, Josephina appeared. "You were too tired when you first came back to make sense. So tell me now, dear. With all the details.

What happened from the moment you arrived there until you came back to the present?"

The story tumbled out. From Amalie's first conversation with Jonathan through her travel back to the past, to their present unhappy situation. Throughout the recitation, Josephina listened quietly. She showed no shock, no disbelief, only occasional sympathetic murmurs or encouraging nods.

Finally, spent, Amalie was at the end of her tale.

For a long time neither of them said anything. Then Josephina spoke. "I must think about this. We know more now than before you made your trip to the past. We must consider what to do next."

"I can't see that there is anything more we can do."

"But Jonathan must still be here for a reason. What if it wasn't meant to have happened like that? What if there was some kind of cosmic error that needs correcting? Perhaps Jonathan wasn't supposed to die at that time, in that way. Perhaps Amalie was supposed to marry him and live to a ripe old age. We don't know that, of course, but it's worth considering."

"I think you're grasping at straws, Josephina. We can't change history."

"Of course we can, dear. They do it all the time in history books."

The next morning, Jonathan was back in the rocking chair, whistling softly when she came out.

"I missed you beside me these last nights. Have I offended you in some way?"

"No, of course not. I thought it unfair. You should have a lover of your own time. One who is flesh and blood. You cannot be satisfied to live the rest of your life with a phantom."

"I think that choice is mine to make. And if it's a choice between you and any man I've ever known, I choose you. I love you, Jonathan. I don't know how we landed in this mess, but of one thing I'm certain. I love you."

"And I love you, both now and in the past. But I can never be any real part of your life here, in this time. No one can see me or even hear me except you."

"Granted. And I know that may cause us problems from time to time." Amalie laughed. "Josephina compared us to couples of different races or different religions. She said we were just of different times."

Jonathan threw back his head and roared. "Trust Josephina to cut through to the heart of the matter. Come, let's walk."

As they trudged through the warm sand he put his arm around her and pulled her close. "I've missed you, too. And I've very much missed being in your bed at night."

Suddenly Amalie's world was brighter.

"I think we should go back, back to the past once more." She stopped and looked fully at him. "We know so much more now than

140

we did before. And knowing might make it possible to change things."

"But how? I've told you that when I'm there I have no knowledge of what's to come. How can we change anything if we don't know what to change?"

"I'll know, Jonathan. I'll remember the way it was and I'll find some way to change things. I'm not sure what to change at this moment, but knowing what will happen if I repeat certain actions, I can try to do things differently."

"What kind of things? What could we have done differently?"

"I'm not sure. But if I hadn't argued with my father, if I hadn't come crying to you the night of my father's ultimatum, perhaps the whole thing might have transpired very differently."

"It doesn't seem likely. He was determined to wed you to Benstone. I could never have countenanced that."

"Let me try, Jonathan. Let me try once more. We know the worst now. Let me try to change the past."

"You're sure you want to do this? For you it's a perilous journey. What if you can't get back to the present?"

Amalie smiled. "Then I might just be stuck in the past with you. I can think of worse things."

Hand in hand they returned to the beach house. Josephina was having her breakfast and feeding crumbs to Enrico. He flapped his wings and flew to the ground as they approached.

141

"There you are. I thought I saw you on the beach. Have some breakfast. Shall I have Elvirna set another place?"

Jonathan smiled. "No thank you. I'm afraid eating is one of life's pleasures definitely denied those of us who live in the aether."

"Never mind. Saves on the grocery bills, I'm sure. Now what have you two been cooking up? I can tell you've decided something."

"We're going back again. We know now what happened, and I think I'll carry that knowledge back with me. Jonathan won't, of course. But perhaps I can change something…"

Josephina beamed at them. "I think that's a wonderful idea. When will you be going?"

Amalie looked at Jonathan, who nodded his agreement.

"Now. I think we'll do it now, before I have time to reconsider."

The thought occurred to Amalie that in altering events of the past, she might well lose her way back to the present. That she could be caught somehow between Jonathan's world and hers. Lost forever in that frightening black vortex she experienced the last time. But she would not burden Jonathan with her fear.

Twenty minutes later they were at Evans Plantation. This time when they stepped through the portal, Jonathan held Amalie close in his arms. As they crossed into the darkness his embrace became tight and solid. Amalie buried her face against his chest as the air whirled

142

around them and the earth disappeared from beneath their feet. They were at first tossed like rag dolls, twisting and turning in the wind, assaulted by its ear splitting howl. Then the rain came. Icy, battering rain. There seemed to be water all around them, a raging frothing inferno, sucking them slowly down, down into a terrifying blackness. Only Jonathan's arms around her kept Amalie from screaming out her fear.

Then, without any transition, they were in Amalie's room at Ansett House. She was in her narrow bed and Jonathan was beside her. She sat bolt upright. "How?" she said loudly, her ears still ringing from the journey.

"Hush, love. Do you want to wake the household? I couldn't sleep. I had such need of you tonight. I climbed the vines to your balcony. I didn't think you'd mind."

Any response Amalie might have made was swallowed by his kiss. She realized he had no memory of the crossing. She wound her arms around his very solid neck and gave herself up to the myriad sensations that followed, one after another in a dizzying progression. He was alive and all male under her hands. She slid her palms over his shoulders and down to his tight muscular buttocks. She moved her hands between his legs and caressed him as he stifled a moan. Finally, able to wait no more, she took his throbbing cock in her hands and guided it into her slippery hot folds. She was blind with her desire for this very real, flesh and blood Jonathan. He gasped and

143

held his breath, willing himself to slow down, to give pleasure, not just to take. Slowly, so slowly, he started to move. Amalie moved with him in the rhythm known by lovers since time immemorial, their tempo increasing, their hearts pounding, until they rose together in a final crashing crescendo. They were one. One in body, mind, and spirit.

Slowly they descended to earth, to the little bed in Amalie's room. They lay exhausted in each other's arms, damp with the sweat of their exertions. Amalie smiled. It was good to be back.

They heard footsteps in the hall. Jonathan slid off the bed onto the floor just as the door opened and Jemma raised her lamp. She looked in and saw Amalie asleep in her crumpled bed. Lowering the lamp, she closed the door. They could hear her retreating footsteps.

Jonathan let out the breath he'd been holding and Amalie smothered her laughter. "By my troth, I've never seen you move that fast, my love."

"You did a fine job of feigning sleep." He kissed the tip of her nose and smoothed her hair. "I love you so, my Amalie. It is long past time we were wed. This is nonsense, this waiting, making love secretly only when we can grasp the moment."

"I know. But you must not come here again. It is much too chancy. I will come to you instead, during the day, when I can get away. Our beach is a much safer refuge for our love making."

"If you insist. Perhaps it is better that way. I tore both my hands and my clothing on the bougainvillea thorns climbing up here tonight. And if Jemma had decided to come in for a closer look…"

He kissed her one last time and was gone, out the balcony doors and down the way he had come. She heard the sound of his mount's hooves recede into the distance as she drifted into exhausted slumber.

The next morning when Jemma awakened Amalie with her morning tea, she looked suspiciously at the bedclothes. "Gonna have to change those. It appear you mighty restless last night."

Amalie smiled innocently. "It was very hot."

"Hmm." Jemma stripped the bed and disappeared out of the door.

Amalie stretched, feeling the effects of last night's lovemaking. His hand on the inside of her thigh had left small purple bruises, his fingers perfectly outlined on her flesh. Funny, she hadn't felt them when he grasped her there to gain fuller entrance to her body. She had better not let Jemma see those. She tingled with remembered passion. Perhaps this afternoon she would be able to slip away.

But what day was it? Last night's experience wasn't one she'd lived through on her first trip to the past. They must have arrived at some earlier point. So much the better, more time in which to formulate a plan.

Jemma returned with her bath water. At Amalie's insistence that she could perfectly well bathe herself, thank you, she huffed to the armoire to lay out Amalie's morning dress.

"Do I have to wear that, Jemma? It's so hot."

"Ladies does not bare they necks and arms before sundown. You knows that."

Amalie sighed and allowed herself to be dressed. First the thin cotton chemise went on, Then Jemma advanced with the whalebone stays.

"No, Jemma. I will not wear those. They are sheer torture. It's bad enough to have to wear them under my evening costume. I will not wear them during the heat of the day."

"Humpf. You so skinny I don't suppose it matter much." Putting the stays aside, Jemma pulled a fine lawn petticoat trimmed with tucks and lace over Amalie's head and began fastening the dozen hooks down the back. Amalie had the fleeting thought that it was no wonder so many women of this time were virtuous. How could they ever get in and out of so much clothing without the help of a ladies maid? Of course there was something to be said for a lover unfastening buttons or hooks, kissing his way down your back as he did so. She gave a small shudder of reminiscence.

"You shivering. Catchin' a cold? I'd best make up my sour-sop and sorrel tonic for you."

"No, Jemma. I'm fine." Her voice was muffled as Jemma pulled the pale yellow muslin gown over her head and smoothed it into place. Jemma buttoned the long sleeves at the wrists, adjusted the high neckline and then attacked the tiny fabric covered buttons that marched down the back of the garment.

Then she pushed Amalie down into the chair at her dressing table and began arranging her hair.

An hour after Jemma had begun the process she declared Amalie ready to leave her room.

Amalie found her father in his study. He turned from his accounts to greet her.

"Good morning, my dear. How lovely you look in that frock."

"Thank you, Papa. What are your plans for today?"

"I must go into town. We need some supplies and I should like to stop and speak with the Administrator."

"Do you suppose I could go with you? I need some embroidery thread and I shouldn't mind an opportunity to visit the Governor's Mansion. We've barely seen Mr. Benstone since he arrived on St. Clement's."

"I was planning to ride, but of course I should be delighted to have your company. I'll have Gerald harness up the curricle."

An hour later they were on their way in the carriage behind two of their smartest looking horses. Her father took the reins while

Amalie, held a parasol open to protect her fair skin from the tropical sun.

Once in town she purchased the embroidery thread she had no need for then accompanied her father to the Governor's Mansion.

They were admitted by a huge, surly-looking man dressed in some sort of quasi-military fashion. With shock, Amalie recognized him. It was Smithins, the man who had murdered Jonathan. She felt chilled in spite of the heat of the day. The man, unaware of her knowledge of a murder he would commit in the future, was addressing them.

"Mr. Benstone suggests that you wait in the library. He will join you there."

Amalie wasn't quite sure why she wanted to meet the Administrator here, on his home ground. She only knew that she needed to find out more about him. What motivated him? Why he was the ruthless killer she knew him to be? She had allowed herself to become a victim last time. This time she would not, not if she could help it. She heard him speak before she saw him and turned to give him a dazzling smile and a slight curtsey.

"Ansett." He shook her father's hand warmly. "I see you've brought your lovely daughter with you. Good day, Mistress Ansett. Welcome to Government House." He lifted her gloved hand to his lips. "Charming." He smiled.

"You are too kind, sir."

Amalie studied him as he turned to talk of business with her father. He was indeed a handsome man, tall, with the appearance of great physical strength. His shoulders seemed to strain at the silk fabric of his waistcoat, yet he exhibited a grace of movement unusual in a man of his size. In this setting, relaxed and talking business with her father, there was no hint of the harsh arrogance she'd seen on her earlier trip to the past. Perhaps his smile didn't quite reach his eyes, but he was cordial as he chatted.

As their business drew to a close, Amalie tuned in to their conversation.

"With regard to the paperwork, it is as I said, safe in my safe." He laughed at his small quip. "And the key is always on my person. But allow me to give you your share of this quarter's profits."

Emile shot a quick look at his daughter, but she had her back to them and appeared to be studying the books on Benstone's bookshelves.

Amalie watched in the mirror beside the bookcase as Benstone extracted a brass key from his left vest pocket and turned to the portrait of the King George the Third hanging behind his desk. Swinging the picture aside, he fitted the key into the lock, opened the safe, and extracted an envelope stuffed with bills, which he handed to Emile Ansett.

"It has been a pleasure doing business with you, Ansett."

Was there the faintest hint of sarcasm in his tone?

149

Her father cleared his throat and gave Amalie a sidelong glance to ensure that she was still otherwise occupied. "Yes. Well. There was just one other thing, you see. I think I should like to withdraw from our joint business venture. That is, if you don't mind."

Benstone's smile was affability itself and his tone was completely friendly. "Oh but I do mind, my dear Emile. In fact, I mind very much. But we must not bore your charming daughter with this. We will discuss it at some later time. Am I still to join you for dinner tonight?"

"Of course. At seven. We shall see you then."

At some unseen signal the thug who had let them in appeared to show them out.

Benstone bent low over Amalie's proffered hand, holding it for just a moment too long before saying, "I shall especially look forward to seeing *you* this evening, Mistress Ansett."

In the carriage on the way home, Amalie tried gently to sound out her father. "What kind of business venture are you engaged in with Mr. Benstone, Papa?

"You mustn't worry your pretty little head about that. Business is a man's affair. As long as I can keep you in new frocks and afford to allow your mother to travel to England, well, that's all you need to know."

Amalie gnashed her teeth, biting back a retort about having run her own successful business for five years in the twenty-first century.

She must remember who she was here and now, although it was very difficult at times.

That afternoon after Jemma had released her from the prison of her morning dress supposedly to take a nap, Amalie put on her brother's clothing so she could slip away to the beach, and to Jonathan. In doing so she realized that she had arrived back to where she had entered on her first visit to the past.

From this moment on she knew exactly what was coming. It was up to her to change it. And she felt sure that the key to changing it lay in Benstone. She needed the key he carried in his vest pocket. She needed the incriminating papers he kept in his safe. And she needed his trust and confidence to get to the key. Or she would have to acquire it by trickery.

On the whole, the latter course seemed more likely. She would begin this evening. She must alter her attitude toward him at every opportunity. She would play the coquette. Be utterly charming. She just hoped Jonathan would understand. She'd explain what she could to him, but how to make him understand when he had no knowledge of the events to come?

While riding through the fields to Evans Plantation her mind chewed on the problem. Her biggest obstacle to what she hoped to accomplish might not be Benstone, but Jonathan. She had a feeling he wouldn't sit idly by while she flirted her way into Benstone's confidence.

151

****

Jonathan turned from where he had been standing by the window as Amalie burst in.

"I just had to see you." Then, seeing the other inhabitant in the room, "Sorry to interrupt you, Samuel."

She waited for him to say, as he had before, "It's no problem, Miss Amalie." But he didn't. He sat looking at her, stunned, as if he were seeing a ghost. His eyes grew wide. If a black face can be said to pale, his did. And his spectacles fell to the floor unnoticed. "Jumbie," he whispered, "Obeah."

Amalie thought, he knows. My God, he knows. She crossed to him, took his hands in hers and looked deeply into his eyes. "It's all right Samuel. I tell you it's all right. I'm here to help." She reached to the floor, retrieved his glasses, and gently placed them back on his face.

He searched her eyes for a moment and then answered. "Good."

"If there is a time when I need you, Samuel, you will help me won't you?" she said softly.

He drew in a quick breath and answered, "Of course I will."

His gaze was glued on her as she and Jonathan left the room.

Jonathan frowned. "What on earth came over Samuel? I've never seen him so shaken."

"He's probably just been working over those books of yours too long. I shouldn't worry about him."

152

That evening, still surfeited by their lovemaking in the afternoon, Amalie took extra pains with her dressing. She knew Benstone would be there. She discarded dress after dress brought out by Jemma until she found one sufficiently daring.

"That too low in the bosom. It show everything but you nipples. Not decent."

"Oh hush, Jemma. Lace me up so I can push my bosom higher. Yes, like that. I want them to look like two round rosy globes above the neckline of my dress."

Emma muttered under her breath, "Round rosy globes. They indecent. What your Papa goin' to say?"

When the diaphanous white gown was settled over Amalie's frame, its tight bodice left little to the imagination. Her breasts were indeed half exposed and the thin fabric did little to hide the remaining half. Under her breasts a wide band of pink silk satin emphasized that which needed no emphasis. The rest of her form was only hinted at, in the style of the day, and the gown stopped just above the floor, revealing her trim ankles, white silk stockings and pink kidskin slippers. Well, thought Amalie, as a dress intended for seduction it ought to do the job. But what was she to do about Jonathan?

She went downstairs.

"Ah, there you are, my dear. Her father stood in the doorway to the parlor as he had before. "Come and greet our guest."

Benstone drew in his breath sharply as she entered the room.

"Good evening, Mr. Benstone. You do us honor by your presence." She curtsied deeply, aware that in doing so she was exposing even more of her breasts than the daring dress already did. She rose slowly, raking her eyes over his figure as she did so. She almost laughed aloud when she saw that he had an erection. This game might prove to be fun.

"You dazzle me with your beauty, Mistress Ansett." He moved to stand behind a chair, no doubt to give himself time to rearrange his clothing.

Jonathan chose that moment to arrive. In the middle of his apology for his lateness he saw Amalie. He stopped mid-sentence and stared. "Good God! What is that you're wearing?" he asked bluntly.

"It's the latest style. Everyone is wearing dresses like this in London and Paris this year."

"But none so charmingly as you, my dear." Benstone's oily voice forestalled the comment on the tip of Jonathan's tongue. "Only recently from London myself, I can tell you that even the infamous Lady Hamilton cannot hold a candle to you."

Benstone appeared unaware of the thunderous look on Jonathan's face.

Amalie smiled in the Administrator's direction and gave a small curtsy once again. "Thank you, kind sir."

She saw that Jonathan was fuming. She would just have to sort it out with him later.

Her father spoke. "I believe dinner is ready. Gentlemen, Amalie." Taking his daughter's arm, he led the small group into the dining room.

When dinner was over, Amalie's father indicated that he wished to meet with the Administrator alone. He spoke to Jonathan. "Perhaps you and Amalie would like to take a turn in the garden. We shall not be long."

"Certainly, sir."

Once out of hearing of the house, Jonathan turned to Amalie and spoke in a low voice, intense with barely controlled anger. "What did you think you were doing in there?"

"Whatever do you mean? Surely you cannot be jealous?"

Jonathan pulled her roughly to him and kissed her deeply. When he released her she could hardly stand. "I'm not jealous. I know you too well for that. You're playing some game of your own. And I want to know what it is. Benstone's no fool. He's unscrupulous and he's meaner than a snake. I don't want you near him."

Amalie studied him. How much could she tell him? Perhaps some part of the truth. "Benstone has some hold over my father. I need to know what it is and to try to remove it."

155

"Hold? What kind of hold?"

"I'm not sure. I think it's something to do with the illicit slave trade."

Jonathan frowned. "That's a nasty business. You can't be involved, whatever is going on. It could be dangerous. You must leave the investigation of this to me."

There it is, Amalie thought. She'd run headlong into that nineteenth century attitude that women were the weaker sex and must at all times be protected. That they mustn't participate in any activity deemed dangerous, or ever initiate any action, except, perhaps, now and then, in bed.

"Of course, dear," she said as demurely as she could manage.

"I mean it, Amalie. Leave Benstone to me. I'll find out what's going on."

And get yourself killed in the process, she thought. Not if she could help it. She reached up and pulled his mouth down to hers, taking his hand and resting it on her breast. It had the effect she had hoped for of driving conscious thought away.

****

The days and weeks passed as they had before, with Amalie slipping away almost daily for her trysts with Jonathan on the beach. Jonathan, as had happened during their last trip to the past, was invited less and less frequently to dine at Ansett House. The Administrator was to the contrary there frequently and Amalie practiced her wiles on him at every opportunity. Now it was he, rather than Jonathan, who strolled with her in the garden after dinner. He made no overt advances, but used every possible opportunity to brush against her, to inadvertently touch her breast as he took her arm. Amalie knew he wanted her and that knowledge gave her a sense of power. Now if she could just figure out how best to use his obvious desire for her.

She knew the date of the murders was advancing rapidly. December tenth. It was emblazoned on her mind. What if, when her father asked her to break off her engagement to Jonathan and accept Benstone, she agreed instead of fighting him? What if she offered no resistance, appeared to embrace the plan? Perhaps she should even anticipate her father's demand.

Her mind raced on. If she didn't confide her suspicions about her pregnancy to Jonathan, he would see no need for their hasty marriage. But how could she protect Jonathan? How could she get him safely out of the way on that fateful night?

Samuel. Samuel could help her. He recognized her as another being, a sort of jumbie in reverse. He saw her for what she was, she was sure of it. And he knew she loved Jonathan as he loved Jonathan. He would help her do whatever was necessary to keep Jonathan safe. She just had to find a way to meet him alone.

The next morning she had her father's groom prepare the larger carriage, the landau. She would need a driver for her purpose today. She then had Jemma dress her for a formal visit to neighbors in a high necked long sleeved morning dress of rose sprigged muslin, with matching parasol, white kid gloves, and to keep off the tropical chill, a shawl. Amalie thought she would suffocate, but she reminded herself of her purpose. Armed with calling cards and small gifts and accompanied by Jemma, since no young lady could make such a trip alone, she started out at ten in the morning.

Her aim was to be at Evans House at one. She knew Jonathan would be in town at that hour, meeting with his banker. He had told her he would be yesterday when they met at the beach. She had to catch Samuel alone.

Of course Evans House wasn't her stated destination. No lady of refinement could visit a bachelor's abode except when surrounded by her family. No. She had told no one that she would be stopping at Evans House.

The social visits were interminable. She smiled until her lips hurt with the artifice and the inane chatter about the weather, the gardens, and old gossip about the Court, always very late in reaching this outpost. It all bored her to tears.

Finally, after the fourth such visit, she turned to Jemma and said, "I think we can go home now." She then instructed the driver, "I'd like to make one short stop on the way. Evans House."

158

To Jemma, who was scowling at this change of plans, she explained, "I left my favorite fan there some weeks ago when we were there for dinner. Jonathan isn't at home this morning, but I should like to stop and pick it up."

At Evans House, she hurried inside and found Samuel where she had hoped he would be, working in the plantation office.

He rose from his desk when she entered. "Jonathan is in town this morning."

She spoke quickly for fear of being interrupted by someone. "I know, Samuel. It's you I need to see."

He nodded. "I've been expecting you. What would you have me do?"

"Jonathan is in grave danger, Samuel, as are you. There is a terrible thing going to happen on December tenth if we don't stop it."

Samuel didn't question her prophesy. "Obeah. You see these things. I knew when I met you last month. You are not Amalie. At least not the Amalie I know. But it is clear you love Jonathan. And whatever you ask of me, I will do."

"Get him away from here, Samuel. Invent some excuse. Get him to travel to St. Luke's or even farther. He's always talking about new experimental crops. Find one that he has to go and investigate. Just get him away from here and go with him. You're in as much danger as he."

He frowned for a moment in thought. "Ananas comosus," he said. "Pineapples. He's been talking about growing pineapples. It seems they are much in demand as a crop, are easy to grow, and are virtually hurricane proof. He's been wanting for some time to visit Antigua where they've been growing them quite successfully. There's a ship in harbor now headed there. I'll strongly suggest that we take this opportunity to go. That should do it."

"Thank you, Samuel. I hope we'll have time to talk more when you return from your trip."

She rushed out of the office, taking a fan out of her reticule as she walked through the front door. The driver helped her into the carriage.

"Here it is," she said to Jemma, opening she fan and using it to stir the breeze. "Now let's go home and have luncheon. I'm famished."

****

Jonathan set sail with Samuel for Antigua on December ninth. Amalie figured that with any luck, he would be gone for a week or longer. That should remove him from danger and give her enough time to carry out the next stage of her plan.

The following evening Amalie dressed with extra care. She wore the most provocative gown she could find in her wardrobe, then sprinkled rosewater on her neck, in her hair, and across the exposed tops of her breasts. She shrugged off the concealing shawl Jemma tried to place about her bare shoulders.

Jemma snorted her disapproval.

"I have to do this Jemma. I'll explain someday."

Then she went downstairs to face the unknown. It began precisely as it had on that fateful December tenth, on her first trip to the past.

When she entered the drawing room she found only Benstone there. She smiled a dimpled smile up at him as she curtseyed low to give him full advantage of the low neckline of her bodice.

Then she strolled out to the terrace, glancing back at him in invitation.

He followed her. "Your father has very kindly allowed me this time alone with you in which to speak."

Amalie smiled. "To speak? Whatever about, my dear Mr. Benstone?"

He raised one eyebrow and his lips curved. "Surely you know about what. It cannot have escaped you attention that my interest in you is more than casual, and I believe by your actions, that my feelings are reciprocated."

"My actions, sir? Whatever do you mean?" Amalie brushed provocatively past him to stand at the edge of the terrace. As she turned to look at him, she parted her lips and wetted them.

"I have the honor to ask you to be my wife, to share my life, my place in the Governor's Mansion."

"Oh. I think I might quite like that." She moved close to him and placed one hand lightly on his chest. "But tell me, sir, how do we seal such a declaration? I've heard tell that it is often with a kiss."

He took both her hands in his and brought his lips down to her fingertips. When she did not break away, or show any sign of disapproval, he chanced kissing her lips. His kiss started softly enough, but it rapidly became fierce, smacking more of possession than of love. She leaned into him rather than resisting as he expected an inexperienced, virginal girl to do. Surprised by her boldness, he began to slide his hands down her body. His fingers skimmed over and around her breasts then down to the rich curves of her buttocks. Once there, he pulled her tight against him so she could not fail to feel his heavy arousal. She gasped as she thought he probably expected her to. Then she brought her hands up to his chest, fumbling with the buttons of his waistcoat, vest and shirt, until her seeking fingers found the wiry curls of his chest hair and threaded her hands through them. He shuddered with sexual excitement and began to pull her skirts up as he deepened the kiss.

His mouth invaded hers as his hands explored her body. Time to stop him, Amalie thought, before it's too late. She bit his lip, hard, not releasing it until she had drawn blood.

He drew back sharply. "Bloody hell!" he exploded. He touched his hands to his mouth and finding blood, took his handkerchief to wipe it away.

Then he burst out laughing. "Ours will be an interesting wedding night, my dear. You have drawn first blood, but I assure you I shall draw second. And you will not find the matter laughable as I find this. I promise you pain, my dear. And I shall enjoy inflicting it upon you, inch by inch by inch." He pulled his clothing back together, then turned and stalked away from her, back into the house.

Emile Ansett came out of his office just as Benstone was leaving.

The Administrator glanced back at Amalie, standing somewhat disheveled and statue still in the drawing room doorway, then bowed slightly toward her father. "Your daughter has just granted me the honor of accepting my proposal of marriage. I think our wedding should be sooner rather than later. I must be in London early in the New Year. I suggest that we should wed on December twenty-sixth, if that is agreeable with you, sir.

Emile Ansett hesitated. "It seems so soon. Her mother…"

"Her mother, I understand, is in London. We shall visit her there."

"Of course." Amalie's father looked at her, confusion written on his features. "If that's what Amalie wants."

When the door was closed on his retreating figure, Amalie smiled a small satisfied smile and glanced down at the key clenched in her hand. It had almost cost her virtue, or what was left of her virtue after two years of making love with Jonathan. But the first two parts of her plan had succeeded. Jonathan was safely away and she had the key to the safe in Benstone's library.

Amalie glanced at her father. His shoulders were slumped and he avoided her gaze. He turned abruptly and went into his study. Frowning, she followed him and found him sitting at his desk, his head in his hands. She went to him and put her arms around him. "What's wrong, Papa?

"I can't help feeling that this is wrong, my dear, you and Benstone. What about Jonathan? You've always planned to marry him."

Amalie's voice hardened. "Plans change. We can hardly be bound by an informal arrangement made when I was little more than a child."

"But you and Jonathan have loved each other since you were sixteen."

"Love is often a poor basis for a marriage. Mr. Benstone can give me rank and position. He's not some struggling planter."

As Amalie threw her father's words from that last visit to the past back into his face, she could see that they didn't resonate in any way with him. Somehow, in changing her behavior she had changed her father's as well.

"It's just that…"

"What, Papa?"

"In marrying Benstone, you will be saving me, saving the family, saving the plantation. If you hadn't made this choice we would have lost everything. Yet I cannot allow you to sacrifice yourself if you are in any way a reluctant bride."

"I don't understand."

"The plantation has been losing money for the last several years. The cost of running it keeps going up and the price of sugar keeps going down."

"I had no idea."

"Sugar cane ceased being a profitable crop some time ago, what with the Napoleonic Wars creating havoc with the shipping lines and then the discovery in Europe that sugar could be made from beets. Jonathan has often told me that I should try alternate crops, but I'm old, and set in my ways."

"But what does Mr. Benstone have to do with any of this? How can my marrying him help?"

Her father sighed, and stood to pace the room. "He has threatened me with exposure. As his future father-in-law, I would be safe. The family will be safe."

"How threatened you with exposure?"

"It was a business arrangement. He persuaded me that by investing my small remaining capital in a shipping deal I could recoup my losses and quadruple my money in a year. I was desperate. I accepted his offer."

Amalie knew what was coming, but she couldn't prevent the chill that ran down her spine. "What kind of shipping business?"

165

"Slaves. We were illegally transporting slaves. After the abolition of the slave trade by England three years ago, there were fortunes to be made in the illicit slave trade."

"Oh, Papa, you didn't! You could go to jail for years. This house, this property could be confiscated."

"Exactly. I tried to get out of the business. I told him that I no longer wished to be a part of his endeavor. I wanted to be free of the slave trade. That with the money I now had, I wanted to do as Jonathan suggested, try other, less labor intensive crops. Crops less reliant on slaves."

"His reply?"

"That mine was the only name on any of the documents pertaining to the illicit trade. That he could, with those documents and a word in the right quarters, see me spend the rest of my life in prison. That my word would mean little against his in any English court. Finally he intimated that as his father-in-law I should of course be safe. That it was all rather up to you. To how you responded to his suit."

Amalie hugged him. "What you did was wrong, but thank you for caring enough to explain it all to me. And you mustn't worry about Mr. Benstone. Everything is going to be all right."

Later that night in her bed, Amalie replayed her conversation with her father. It had differed in significant ways from the time before, when he had ordered her marriage to Benstone. She was correct in

166

her supposition that by changing her own behavior she could alter the events around her.

But the greatest challenge lay ahead. Somehow she had to retrieve the incriminating papers from the safe and destroy them. Then she had to face Benstone. She didn't think he would accept defeat at the hands of a woman lightly.

CHAPTER 8

It was noon when Benstone arrived. Amalie had been expecting him. It was too much to hope for that he would not have noticed the missing key. Over Jemma's strong objections, she had dressed in a low cut frock of the type not usually worn before sunset. She would need to provide all the distraction she could if she wanted to divert his attention from the missing key.

"Good day, Mr. Benstone. We weren't expecting you, although I must say I am most happy to see you. You left somewhat hurriedly last evening." Amalie smiled up at him.

"Good day, Mistress Ansett. You look charming, as always. But I seem to have misplaced something last evening. I wonder if you may perhaps have found a brass key?"

Amalie frowned in pretended thought. "You lost a key? But however could that have happened? Where do you think you lost it?"

He gave her a wintery smile. "It had occurred to me that when we were alone on the terrace or in the drawing room..."

"I can assure you, Mr. Benstone, that my mind was not on such trifles as keys last evening." She laughed a low seductive laugh. "If you lost a key somehow when we were," she paused as if to seek a delicate way of expressing it, "otherwise engaged, I'm afraid I was in no condition to notice it. I'm afraid your…" again she paused so that his imagination could fill in the blank, "declaration… left me quite breathless."

He laughed mirthlessly. "It left me with a sore lip."

"For that I am most sorry. I cannot begin to imagine whatever came over me."

"Perhaps we could go to the drawing room and terrace to look. It may simply have dropped out of the pocket of my vest. I seem to recall that somehow both my waistcoat and my vest came unbuttoned."

Amalie managed to feign a blush, and eyes down, answered, "Of course we must look. And I will speak to the girl who cleaned the room this morning. Perhaps she will have found it."

She led the way to the terrace and then to the drawing room and made a show of checking beneath the pillows of the settee and under the chairs, while Benstone stood watching her, suspicion in his eyes.

Then she pulled the bell chord for the maid, who of course had found nothing.

"I'm sorry I cannot help you further. Was this key of any importance?"

"Of course it was important. Otherwise why would I be here?" His voice was laced with sarcasm.

"I had rather hoped that you might have wished to see me."

His eyes raked over her, taking her in fully for the first time that morning. "While I should like very much to take up where we left off last evening, I'm afraid I have a meeting in town. Still, a brief kiss perhaps, a token of what is to come, my dear."

Amalie closed her eyes and chastely lifted her closed lips to him. He placed his hands on her arms, pulled her roughly toward him and skimming past her lips, bit her breast hard through the thin fabric of her dress.

Amalie, who had thought until this moment that she was fully in control of the situation, gasped in pain and outrage. "Bastard!"

He laughed. "That's more like it. If I had thought you to be the prissy little piece you presented to me this morning, I should never have asked you to be my wife. I am going to enjoy taking your virginity, my dear. I shan't pretend that you will enjoy it, but I shall."

With that he stalked out of the room and out of the house.

Amalie was fuming. What a prick! Virginity indeed. He was not just a sadist, he was a stupid sadist. She filed the thought away for future reference.

Then she looked down at herself. She had thought she was doing such a good job of playing the nineteenth century ninny. Clearly the twenty-first century crept through when she least expected it. Still, she had considerable respect for her ancestor. How did she ever navigate these treacherous waters? Women had so little control over their destinies in those days. Between their fathers and their husbands, it was a wonder any of them survived. Then her thoughts turned to Jonathan. A good man was a good man, whatever the century. She supposed that made all the difference. She went to her room to change her clothing and to dress the wound on her left breast.

December eleventh. The horrific events of that other December tenth had not happened. Jonathan was still alive. Samuel was with him. And Amalie, both of today and yesterday, was still here, still in possession of her sanity. She was weak with relief.

Jonathan had been gone two days. He would probably arrive in Antigua this afternoon. It would take a couple of days to investigate the pineapple crop and make whatever arrangements he needed for purchase and transport of the plants. He wouldn't be heading home until that was done. It wasn't every day that a schooner came to St. Clement's from Antigua. She should have at least ten days in which to break into Benstone's safe, Amalie thought. She shivered when she thought about Benstone. It would not do to be discovered in the act of theft. He was a big man, strong and…what had Jonathan said? *Mean as a snake*. It wasn't that she was afraid of him. Not exactly. Still it would be better if he were not in the Governor's Mansion on the night she tried to burgle it.

Carefully she put out feelers. She sent a note inviting him to dinner on the following evening. He accepted. That was of no use.

171

She couldn't burgle his office while entertaining him at dinner. She endured the evening. At least she didn't have to put up with his advances. She had warned her father that she did not wish to be alone with the Mr. Benstone on that occasion and her father, unquestioningly, had never left her side.

While Benstone was there, she broached the subject of his availability during the coming weeks. "I feel we should get to know one another better before our upcoming nuptials, sir. The more we can see of each other, the easier the adjustment will be to my wifely duties." She spoke meekly and with downcast eyes.

She felt rather than saw his amused disbelief. "Of course, my dear. I am at your disposal. I can be with you any evening except next Tuesday. On that evening I have promised to attend a dinner at the officers' barracks."

Bingo! Tuesday was cutting it a little fine, but Jonathan was unlikely to be back that soon.

As the night approached, Amalie was filled with apprehension. Perhaps she should wait until Jonathan returned. If she were to be discovered the consequences would be dire, of that she had no doubt. He would not be summoning the police. No, Benstone would make her pay for her duplicity in some slow and painful way. Still, he had murdered Jonathan the last time. She could not risk a repetition of that. She tried to tell herself that she was in no danger from Benstone but still the cloud of worry hovered.

Finally it was Tuesday. She knew his dinner invitation was for eight. She decided that she should conceal herself outside the Governor's mansion in time to see him leave, just to be certain that he was not unexpectedly at home. There was a wall surrounding the garden. It would offer protection against discovery.

Apologizing to her father that she had a headache and was not up to dinner, she dismissed a suspicious Jemma for the evening and proceeded to dress in her brother's clothing. As a finishing touch she smeared her face and hands with lamp black, and tucked her long pale hair into a cap. She needed to blend with the shadows until time for the break-in.

Mounting her mare, taking first the paths through the fields and then the back lanes, she rode into town. She tethered Molly behind the Anglican Church where she could retrieve her quickly once the job was finished. Then she climbed over the stone wall to wait.

Shortly before eight she heard him leave. "I shan't be needing you further this evening, Smithins. You need not attend me when I return. I shall no doubt be late."

"Very well, sir."

The voice sent a chill down Amalie's spine.

She waited another hour. It was important the household be quiet. Finally she moved. She went directly to the French doors leading from the garden to the Benstone's office. They were unlocked as she had expected them to be. Even in the twenty-first century, no one

173

locked their doors on St. Clement's. She opened the doors and stepped in, closing them quietly behind her. She stood still until her eyes adjusted to the dark. Then went to the portrait covering the safe and pulled it aside.

****

It had been a most successful trip, Jonathan thought as he descended the gangplank at sundown. They had bought three hundred pineapple plants and managed to find a sloop headed for St. Clement's that very same day. He was anxious to see Amalie. His arms ached to hold her. But first he must go home and bathe. He stank of the cargo of fish the boat had been carrying and he hadn't shaved in forty-eight hours. No. He'd best make himself presentable before seeing her. And a good night's sleep might help as well. He'd call on her directly tomorrow morning.

Once at home and cleaned up, he crawled between his sheets. It was an early hour for bed, but he'd been long without sleep. He lay staring at the ceiling. Try as he would, sleep would not come. In its place came images of Amalie. Amalie running into the sea, her pale hair flashing in the sunlight, Amalie cutting flowers from the garden to grace the rooms of Ansett Plantation, Amalie under him in her little bed.

God's breath! How could he sleep? He was fully aroused. He got out of bed and threw on fresh clothes. She had told him not to climb to her balcony again, but surely it could do no harm, just this one last time. She would welcome him, he was sure. He was determined there would be no more waiting. They would wed before Christmas. He would speak to her father tomorrow. They could always have a second ceremony if her mother wished it when she returned from London. This sneaking around was not to his liking, not at all.

A half hour later he stood in her room, staring at her empty bed. It wasn't late, but the house was dark. Dinner was over and except for a light in her father's office, Jonathan had seen no signs of life in the household. Where was she?

At that moment the door opened and Jemma held up her oil lamp. She drew in her breath on seeing him. Her eyes went quickly to the bed. "Where's Amalie?"

"Suppose you tell me. What's going on here?" He pulled her into the room and shut the door.

Jemma started to cry. "She so different. I don't know what she thinkin' to get herself engage to that man."

"What man? What are you talking about, Jemma? Where's Amalie?"

"I ain't know. Just she say she have a headache. She never have a headache. I knows she up to something. She gone to that man. I knows it."

"Jemma, what man?" Jonathan tried not to shout.

"That Benstone man. The Administrator. She say she gonna marry he."

175

Jonathan pushed past Jemma and down the stairs to Emile Ansett's office. Amalie's father looked up to see seething rage in Jonathan's face.

"What...?"

"Where is Amalie?"

"Upstairs in her room. She had a headache."

"She's not there."

"She's not in her room?" Emile Ansett wrung his hands, his voice edged with hysteria. "Oh, God. What's she doing? I was afraid she might do something rash. I suspected that this engagement to Benstone was part of some wild scheme of hers to save me."

Jonathan spoke through gritted teeth. "You think she has gone to the Governor's Mansion? Alone? At this hour of the night? To save you from... what? Never mind. Tell me on the way. We must get there quickly. God only knows what he may do to her if he suspects her of duplicity."

The two men rode hard into town.

Amalie tried to fit the key into the door of the safe. Her hands were slippery with sweat and the key fell to the floor. As she stooped behind the desk to retrieve it, the door to the library opened abruptly and lamplight spilled into the room. She realized that the portrait over the safe was swung wide. She held her breath, terror freezing her to the spot.

"What the devil?" Benstone's voice filled the room. In two strides he was at his desk. He pulled her up roughly.

"Just what do you think you're doing, boy?" He shook her like a rag doll and her cap fell off, her bright hair tumbling down around her shoulders.

"Amalie!" He sat down abruptly, staring at her, still grasping her arms in a vise-like grip.

Amalie tried to control her voice. Not to show the terror she was feeling. "I want those papers. The ones you have incriminating my father."

"So that's what this has all been about. All your seductive ways. I knew you were after something. I thought it was marriage and social position."

"Marriage to you?" Amalie's voice was scathing.

"No?" He gave her a speculative look. "Well, now we know what you want. That brings us to what I might want. Your face is dirty, as are your hands, but perhaps you felt no need to blacken…"

Without warning he put his hand in the neckline of her shirt and ripped it to her waist. "Ah. No lamp black here. All white and clean. I see the marks of my recent kiss are healing nicely."

He reached into his desk with one hand and extracted a length of chord. He pulled Amalie's hands roughly behind her back and secured them with it.

Amalie twisted in his grasp trying to gain some measure of control.

"Enough!" He spun her around so that she was once again facing him. "You are helpless here. The sooner you realize that fact the easier it will be for you. Although I have little desire at this moment to make this at all easy for you. No. I think I should like to make you pay for this indignity in a number of interesting ways."

"Men who are uncertain of their manhood often issue such threats. I'm not afraid of you." Amalie wasn't at all sure that was true, but just saying it made her feel better.

"Bitch! I will teach you a lesson about manhood you won't soon forget." He tugged at the drawstring of her brother's drawers and they fell in a puddle at her feet. He then ripped through the thin fabric of her chemise, leaving her standing before him, naked and shivering.

"Cold, my dear? I think I can correct that." He groped her sex roughly with one hand while squeezing and twisting an exposed breast with the other.

Amalie bit her lip to keep from crying out. She sensed that to scream would be of no use in this household, and it would give him pleasure. For the moment, she would have to endure, but surely at some point in this sick game he would be vulnerable. And at that moment she would make her escape. He hadn't bound her feet.

He removed his hands from her and stood back to better see her face. She tried to keep her expression neutral.

"What, my dear? You are so soon bored with our games? I assure you, we have just begun."

He reached into his desk again, this time pulling out a leather strap. "I think before we go any farther with this you must understand fully what your position is. Swiftly her threw her across his desk, face down, and brought the strap smartly down with a loud snap across her buttocks.

She had to get out of here before he killed her. Quickly she righted herself and ran for the door. Grasping the knob awkwardly with her bound hands, she flung it open to find Smithins standing in her path, his gaze somewhere above her head, his face impassive.

She screamed and slowly backed up.

"Would you like my assistance, sir? Perhaps I could hold her down."

"I don't think that will be necessary, Smithins. Will it Amalie?"

She drew in her breath sharply.

"No." Benstone smiled. "I didn't think you would find that necessary."

Amalie backed slowly away from the assassin.

"Close the door, Smithins."

"Yes, sir.

Benstone towered over her. "I see the lesson has not yet been fully learned. That's not a problem. I'm a patient teacher."

He took her by her bound wrists and dragged her across the room, throwing her once again across his desk. He brought the strap down smartly. Amalie cried out as she felt her flesh tear under the blow

"Ah. So we have found our voice. Good."

After that there was just the haze of pain, until her world was reduced to red, enveloping agony.

Finally the blows stopped. She shuddered. She had survived. She hurt, oh God, how she hurt. But she was alive. Surely the worst was over.

"Good. We'll just try again now that you know who is in charge." He turned her around so that she was forced to watch him unbutton his pants. His engorged phallus burst forth. It was huge.

"You were saying about my manhood?"

He pushed her down across the desk once more, roughly pulled her legs wide and said, "Now let us just see how difficult for you we can make the taking of your maidenhead."

Through the haze of pain, Amalie laughed. "You are too late for that by about two years, sir."

"What? What did you say?" He pulled her up to face him. "What did you say?"

Amalie realized with a start that he had lost his erection. She looked at his limp member and without thinking about the possible consequences, she laughed. And having started laughing was unable to stop.

"Strumpet!"

Jonathan burst into the room as Benstone struck Amalie a powerful blow with the back of his hand, knocking her off his desk and into the sharp edge of the marble topped library table beside it.

"Amalie!" Jonathan's rushed to where she had fallen. He knelt down and gathered her into his arms. Blood was gushing out of the deep wound in her head, wetting his clothing. "Amalie." His voice was filled with anguish.

"I knew you would come." Her voice faded, and with a shudder, her breathing ceased.

"Amalie, no!" There was utter desolation in the cry. Jonathan cradled her head in his hands and, weeping, kissed her dead lips. Then he covered her with his cloak and put her gently down.

"Benstone." Death was in Jonathan's eyes as he stood and looked at Amalie's killer. He walked slowly toward the man who had taken away his reason for living, oblivious to everything except his need to exact vengeance. He didn't hear the other man enter the room silently behind him. And when the knife entered his back he hardly felt it. As if in slow motion he collapsed.

Benstone straightened his clothing and turned to his valet. "Was there anyone with him?"

"Her father," Smithins answered.

"And?"

"Dead. What do you want me to do with the bodies?"

"Take them all to Evans Plantation. Put the bodies in the drawing room and set fire to the place. We'll put it down to a slave uprising. That man of Evans'? Samuel? We'll blame it on him."

Benstone looked at the body of Amalie, sprawled on the floor. "Pity. I think she'd have made a most satisfactory wife."

Huddled in the corner shaking uncontrollably, the other Amalie, unseen, unheard, sobbed. She had made a difference this time. Indeed. There were now three people dead rather than two, because of her arrogance, because of her belief that she could change the past.

CHAPTER 9

Amalie had no recollection later of leaving that place of death and destruction. She supposed that she must have been in shock. Josephina found her on the veranda, huddled over in physical and emotional pain, gulping for breath between tears. She took her wordlessly up to her room.

"Lie down, dear. Get into bed."

"I can't lie down. Don't you understand? I hurt too much."

Amalie paced the small room, not looking at Josephina, trying to talk through her mounting hysteria. "I was the one who took the punishment. Not the other Amalie. Only I. Thank God for that. She didn't suffer. She died, but she didn't have to endure the pain and fear. Only I did."

Josephina waited.

Amalie pulled her clothing aside to show the marks and purple bruises on her breasts and the raw strap marks on her buttocks and back.

Josephina drew in her breath sharply. "We must clean and dress those wounds."

Amalie continued as if she had not heard. "She didn't feel this when it happened. Only I did. When he discovered us there in his study, we fought for control, that other Amalie and I, and I won. I pushed her aside. But she took possession again just before the blow that killed her. I was laughing, uncontrollably, and in that moment she took over our body. She pushed me out. I looked at her before they took her away. There were no marks on her body. This pain was mine alone, and I am glad. I could not have borne knowing I brought that upon her."

Josephina absorbed Amalie's incredible confession without comment, and said, "Drink. Drink and sleep." She put two small pills in Amalie's hands and watched her down them obediently.

"Good. Now I'll clean the wounds on your back and put some salve on them. Strictly speaking we should call the doctor, but I can't begin to imagine how we could explain the situation."

A half hour later, Josephina smoothed her hand over Amalie's hair and said, "We'll talk later. Tomorrow will be time enough." Then she sat in the chair in the corner of the room. She did not leave until Amalie was asleep.

That night Amalie dreamed that Jonathan was with her. He surrounded her with clouds of soft air. He moved his hands over her, cooling, healing, taking away the pain. He kept whispering the same words over and over. "My love, my brave, foolish love."

184

In the morning Amalie awoke feeling refreshed. She jumped out of bed, thinking to take a swim before breakfast. She was reaching for her swim suit when the past came crashing in on her. She sat down abruptly.

She looked at her body. The bruises on her breasts were gone. Not just faded, gone. She stood and looked at her back in the mirror. Not a mark.

Jonathan. Jonathan had been there during the night. He had taken away the marks of the past. The physical pain. Now if only he could take away the mental anguish of what she'd brought about.

She slipped into her suit and went down to the beach. She felt the need of the cleansing cooling waters of the sea. She floated weightlessly for a time, emptying her mind of everything except the gentle rolling waves and the cloudless sky.

Finally she headed for shore. As she stepped out on the sun warmed sand she realized Jonathan was beside her. She leaned into him, tears wetting her cheeks.

He enveloped her with his warmth and spoke. "You were not at fault, my love. You were incredibly brave. Foolish? Yes. But what have we lost?"

"How can you say that? We have lost everything. Amalie died. You died. Samuel was to be tried for your murder. What did we accomplish?"

185

"What was the date of my passing the first time?"

"December tenth."

"And this time?

"December fourteenth."

"And of Amalie's death the first time?"

"It was seven months later."

"And the second time?"

"December fourteenth, eighteen ten."

"And wasn't Amalie's death this time preferable to the way she died the first time? She never married Benstone. Can you even imagine what horrors that saved her?"

Amalie's eyes widened. She had not even thought about what those seven months of marriage to a sadist must have been like for her ancestor.

"Amalie, don't you see. We've changed history. This wasn't the outcome we hoped for, but the past we created is preferable to the past that was."

Later that day she gave Josephina a highly edited version of the events of their second trip to the past.

Josephina's response was one Amalie had not expected. "We must go to the museum, first thing tomorrow morning."

"The museum?"

"To see the portraits."

"I see. You think they will be different now."

186

"If the first Amalie never married Benstone…"

"Of course. How could I not have considered that?"

"And then we must go to the old Anglican cemetery."

"How clever you are, Josephina. I should never have thought of either of those things. The old newspaper reports will be different, too, I imagine. We shall see."

"And how is your back today? Perhaps I should put salve on it again. I'm still not certain we shouldn't take you to see the doctor."

"It's completely healed. There is no mark of any kind. No pain." Amalie paused. "Jonathan visited me last night. He…, I'm not sure what he did. But it left me completely healed."

"My. What a useful talent in a lover."

Amalie burst out laughing. God, it felt good to laugh.

Their visits to the museum and the cemetery the next morning proved very informative. Benstone's portrait still hung in the drawing room, but Amalie's was missing.

Josephina smiled and said, "Changing history, it's a satisfying thing."

Near the portrait was a glass show case. In it, among shards of antique china, clay pipe stems, and slave beads lay a tarnished brass key.

Amalie drew in a shocked breath. It couldn't be. And yet…She asked Gustavia about it.

"It's to the old safe in the wall behind the painting of George the Third in the drawing room. Of course there's nothing in the safe and it's so rusted we could probably never open it at this point, but we kept the key and put it on display. After all, it was hand forged."

"I see. Do you suppose I could borrow it briefly?"

Gustavia looked at Josephina questioningly.

"I'll take responsibility for it. I'm sure Amalie has a good reason for wanting to keep it for a little while."

"Of course."

"Thank you, Gustavia. Now Amalie and I would like to spend some time in the archives if it's convenient."

The old newspaper story was much as it had been, about a slave uprising and the murders of Jonathan Evans and Emile Ansett, except that now Amalie's name appeared alongside her father's and her lover's. The greatest difference in the story was that Samuel was neither hung nor shot while trying to escape. It seemed that he evaded capture and escaped to the hills.

"Good for you, Samuel," Amalie said aloud.

In the cemetery, they found the first Amalie's grave close beside her father's, and Jonathan's a short distance from them. The dates on all had changed.

"You know what this means, Amalie," Josephina said as they played cribbage that evening. "If you can change the past once, you can change it again. You just have to keep trying. But the next time you must not act alone."

"I'm not sure what you mean, Josephina."

"You cannot close out the first Amalie or exclude Jonathan from your plans. That was wrong of you. And Jonathan's friend, Samuel. It seems to me that he could be a very great help if you allowed him to be. You said he seemed to sense that you were – what on earth can we call you – a future jumbie, I suppose. A spirit from another time. If he recognizes that, he could be infinitely useful."

"He seemed actually afraid when he first looked at me, Josephina. And he said a word, 'obeah' I think it was. Do you know what that means?"

"Indeed. One cannot have lived eighty-five years in the West Indies without knowing about Obeah. It is a form of black magic that was old long before the Caribbean was even discovered. When the slaves were transported to the West Indies from Africa, they brought their religion, Obeah, with them. Even today Obeah is much more widely practiced than most people suspect."

"But what is it?"

"Among other things, it is a belief in magic, in the power of certain people among them to work spells."

"Spells? Do you mean…"

"To bring about supernatural intervention, if you will. The Obeah practitioner on an island is the person people turn to when other channels fail. It is believed that he or she can provide magic potions and weave spells. These can be used for many purposes. To make the object of love fall in love, to exact revenge for a real or imagined wrong, even to cure a so-called incurable disease. There are many uses for Obeah."

"But that's just superstition. Surely it's not practiced here in the twenty-first century?"

"The young are perhaps more skeptical. After all this is the age of computers and iPhones. But I can assure you the practice is not dead. As recently as twenty years ago there was an Obeah death on St. Clement's. A man died as a result of an Obeah man giving him a way to break the spell another man had put on him. Unfortunately, the potion given to break the spell contained arsenic. The man was found amidst a mess of chicken feathers, candle wax, and blood. No one was ever prosecuted. The Obeah man was from another island, but even if he had not been, no one would have arrested him. Everyone was too afraid of the consequences."

"But that's bizarre. Everyone I've met here goes to church. There are a dozen different churches on this small island."

"Christianity is practiced alongside of Obeah. The West Indian sees no conflict in that. Are the two really so different? In the world of Christianity, do young girls not pray to the Virgin to make the beloved notice them? Do the sick not travel to Lourdes hoping for a miracle?"

Amalie was silent, trying to absorb the enormity of what Josephina had just told her. Finally she said, "Samuel. He thought I was capable of working spells? That I was an Obeah woman?"

"I suspect that's exactly what he thought. And if you aren't, what are you? How else can you explain your inhabiting the body of someone else? Of course, Samuel must have strong Obeah powers himself, to have recognized that in you."

"You speak of Obeah as if you believe in it."

"Amalie, I'm eight-five years old. I've seen many things in all those years. I see before me my beloved cousin struggling daily with her love for a man who died two hundred years ago. I believe anything is possible."

****

Night after night, Amalie had nightmares. Only Jonathan's presence in her bed kept her from living and reliving those last hours. When she stared moaning in her sleep he would wake her with soft kisses and would caress her until sensation overtook fear and she could give herself up to the passion she felt for him. After he made love to her, invariably she slept soundly and dreamlessly until morning.

Gradually the nightmares faded and their lives took on some semblance of normalcy. That is, Amalie thought, as normal as could be expected when one had a ghost for a lover. It was difficult at times to think of Jonathan as a phantom when he seemed so real to

191

her. And it didn't help that Josephina treated him as a member of the family. When Elvirna wasn't around to hear her, she would seek his advice on the most absurd things.

"Jonathan, I'm thinking of having this cushion recovered. Which of these fabrics do you like better?"

He would consider gravely. "The blue, I think."

Or, "I can't decide whether to put another hibiscus in here at the foot of the steps, or to try poinsettia. What do you think?"

"The hibiscus will do better in that spot. The poinsettia gets a bit leggy."

Then, out of the blue, "So when are you going back? You two have unfinished business with Benstone, I think."

Amalie caught her breath.

Jonathan spoke. "I'm not sure we are going back. I don't think I can put Amalie though that again."

****

One morning, about a month after their return, Elvirna rushed out to the veranda where Amalie was enjoying her first cup of coffee.

"I can't rouse Miss Josephina. She don't answer."

Amalie ran back to Josephina's room then walked slowly over to the bed. Josephina looked like she was asleep. Her face was relaxed and somehow younger looking. But she was no longer there.

Amalie lifted her cousin's hand to her lips and kissed it. She swallowed the sob that threatened to escape. "Oh, Josephina, I had

192

you for such a short time. Why did you have to go and leave me when there was so much I wanted to ask you about? When there was so much still to share?" She smoothed the older woman's hair back and turned to Elvirna. "She's gone. You'd best call the doctor."

Tears streamed down Elvirna's cheeks as she left the room to follow Amalie's instructions, muttering, "She never listen. I try to keep she in bed, but she never listen."

"Don't blame yourself, Elvirna. Josephina lived the way she wanted to. And I suspect she died the way she wanted to."

Back in her room Amalie took out her cell phone. "Lorna, Josephina, she…" She broke down, unable to say another word. She cried as she hadn't cried since her mother's death. All the sorrow of the past five years poured out.

Lorna waited for the storm to pass. Then she said, "I'm so sorry, Amalie. She was a wonderful old lady and I know how much you've come to love her. I'll be on the next plane."

The Anglican Church was full to overflowing for Josephina Ansett's funeral. Those who couldn't fit inside waited outside and went to the second, shorter service at the graveside. Many people spoke of her, of her generosity, of her kindness, of her gentle loving disposition. When it was Amalie's turn to speak, she wasn't sure she could. But then the words came.

"You've all known Josephina so much longer than I. But if I had known her for a lifetime I could not have loved her more. She had a way of shedding light on life's problems, big and small, of creating laughter out of sadness. She had the gift of joy and it was a gift she shared with everyone. I know I'm richer for having known her. I shall miss her deeply."

When Amalie sat down, Lorna took her hand.

****

After the funeral service at the Anglican Church and grave side service Amalie and Lorna went back to the beach house where it seemed the whole island arrived in a steady stream to express condolences, to speak of their affection for this grand old lady, the last of the St.Clement's Ansetts. Most came carrying gifts of food that Elvirna somehow found room for on tables in the kitchen, the parlor, and the veranda.

It was long after dark when the last of the mourners left. At the end, a very tall, dignified black man, dressed in a dark suit and tie spoke to Amalie.

"I'm Edward Sloan. We haven't met but I knew your cousin well. I just wish I could have met you under happier circumstances. I should like an appointment to get together with you as soon as possible. I'll need to see Elvirna and Andrew Jones as well. And Father Peter and Gustavia Graham."

Puzzled, Amalie said, "What's this about?"

194

"Sorry. I should have explained. I'm Josephina's solicitor. It's about her will. Josephina made a new will a few weeks ago and you're a beneficiary, as are the others I mentioned. My office is a bit small. Do you think we could meet here?"

Somewhat confused, Amalie replied, "I suppose we can."

"Thank you. That will be a great help. And would tomorrow morning be convenient? Say ten o'clock?"

"Ten will be fine."

Lorna came to join Amalie in the doorway and gazed at Edward Sloan's departing figure. "Who was that very attractive man I saw you talking with a few minutes ago?"

"He said he was Josephina's solicitor and that she has left me something in her will. How like her to remember me. I suspect she has left me that lithograph." Amalie nodded toward the picture of the plantation house on the wall. "She knew how I loved it."

Lorna studied the picture without comment.

****

The next morning at dawn, unable to sleep, Amalie went for a walk on the beach. Jonathan joined her as she had prayed he would.

"She has passed over. She's happy and at peace," he said. "She'll never roam as I do. She'll join her Jeremy now."

"Jeremy?"

"When she was seventeen, her lover was lost at sea. She never looked at another man."

195

"She never said…"

"Josephina wasn't always old, you know. Once she was young and in love. She was much like you."

Amalie smiled. "You know, when she spoke to me about you it was in the same way she spoke of everyone. I believe she thought of you as just another neighbor."

"Even years ago she was aware of my presence. Until you came, she didn't exactly see me, not as you see me. To her I was a spirit, something nebulous. But she always knew when I was with her. She was never afraid of me as most people are."

"She said it was because she was an Ansett."

"She told you that?"

"Yes. From the beginning, she knew I could see you and talk with you in a way no one else could. She said it was because I was so like the other Amalie. She said other things, too. We'll talk about them when all this is over."

A voice called down from the veranda. "Amalie? What are you doing out there? Wait. I'll join you."

Jonathan faded into nothingness as Lorna came running down the steps to the beach. "Isn't it a glorious day? I thought I heard you talking to someone. Have you taken to conversing with yourself?"

Amalie laughed. "No. Not really. Just ruminating."

"I'm starved. Let's get some breakfast before your handsome Mr. Sloan arrives."

Two hours later they were all convened in the parlor. Elvirna and Andrew, Father Peter, Gustavia Graham, Amalie, Lorna, and Edward Sloan.

"Do you mind if my friend, Lorna, remains here with me?"

"No. No, of course not." Edward Sloan gave Lorna an appraising look. Lorna turned her full wattage smile on him, and apparently confused, he found refuge quickly in the papers in front of him. "Yes. Well. I guess we're all here. I have in front of me Josephina Christina Ansett's last will and testament, duly signed and witnessed. It's a very straightforward document."

He looked first at the Anglican priest. "To the church, she leaves the sum of thirty thousand pounds."

Father Peter gasped. "How very generous. I had no idea…"

"To the Historical Society, she likewise leaves the sum of thirty thousand pounds."

Gustavia Graham smiled. "That will support the museum for years. She always said she'd remember the Historical Society in her will, but this is far beyond expectations."

"To my friends and lifelong companions Elvirna and Andrew Jones, I leave the sum of fifty thousand pounds and an annuity that will continue their salaries for as long as they live. I also leave them the title to the house in town that they have occupied since they were married. And a final instruction to Andrew that he is to go get that cataract surgery."

Elvirna collapsed in tears on her husband's shoulder. Andrew said, "I'll do that Miss Josephina."

"The balance of my estate, I leave to my beloved cousin Amalie Ansett."

"Oh, no. She didn't…she couldn't…" Amalie looked at the solicitor in stunned disbelief. "Do you mean to say that Ansett Beach House is mine?"

"All of the Ansett properties. You now own Ansett Beach House. You also own the ruin that is known as Ansett Plantation and approximately half of the lower slopes of Mt. Zingara. There is also a small trust fund. Enough annually to cover the taxes and then some, I expect."

"I can't believe it." She turned to Lorna.

"Believe it." Lorna replied. "I'm not surprised. She loved you. And she considered you the future of this place. Who else would she have left it to?"

Later, when the crowd had left, Amalie and Lorna sat in the rocking chairs on the veranda and gazed at the sea.

Lorna broke the silence. "I knew you wouldn't be coming back. It's all right. Stephanie is working out well in the office and it hasn't done us any harm to have you working from here. If I get to come to the Caribbean three or four times a year for business consultations with you, that's hardly a bad thing."

"Thank you for understanding, Lorna. I'm glad I still have a job. I don't know how I'd support this place otherwise."

"What was all that about Ansett Plantation and Mt. Zingara? I know that giant of an extinct volcano is called Mt. Zingara, but Ansett Plantation? You never mentioned that."

"It's a ruin, Lorna. Old brick and stone walls covered with vines. No roof. There's a tree growing out of the foundation. The place dates from the late seventeen hundreds."

"And the land Mr. Sloan spoke about?"

"It's the old sugar cane plantation land. I suppose there's a lot of it. It climbs up the mountain behind the ruins of the manor house."

"I'd like to see it. Can we go tomorrow?"

Amalie hesitated. Why was she afraid to show the place to Lorna? It was ridiculous. She wouldn't accidentally slip back into the past. Would she? Not if Jonathan wasn't with her.

"Of course we can go there tomorrow. But there's not much to see. Wear closed shoes. The bush is dense."

On the drive out to Ansett Plantation the next day, Lorna commented on the lack of houses. "Considering how many locals and expats live on the rest of this island, how come no one has chosen to build out here? It's gorgeous. All those vistas of sea. That spectacular view of St. Kitts on the horizon. It's the most scenic spot I've seen yet on St. Clement's."

"There's no electricity out here."

199

"Surely that shouldn't be an insurmountable problem."

Amalie took a deep breath. "It's haunted."

Lorna burst out laughing.

"Laugh if you like, but no local is going to build out here."

"Are you serious?"

"Have you never considered that maybe, just maybe, there might be such a thing as ghosts, spirits, or, as they are known in the Caribbean, jumbies?"

"Can't say as I have. And if you're thinking along those lines, Amalie, you've been here too long."

Amalie sighed. She loved Lorna, but she couldn't possibly tell her about Jonathan. She would never understand.

"Here we are." She pulled over to the side of the road.

Lorna jumped out of the jeep and strode over to the old walls. She stood and stared for a moment in silence. Then she turned to Amalie. "This place must have been magnificent in its day."

"It was. It was a large house, built of stone and clapboard." She gestured. "Outside, balconies ringed the second floor. There were floor to ceiling windows and wide verandas covered with bougainvillea. The front doors opened to a wide center hallway with parquet flooring and high ceilings and a curving staircase. There was a gigantic chandelier. In the evenings, its candlelight would spill out on the gardens. The other Amalie would sing Greensleeves and accompany herself on the pianoforte." She sighed. "It was another way of life."

"That's quite a picture you paint. It's almost as if you had been there."

Amalie brought herself back to the present sharply. "At least that's what Josephina used to say."

"She had a vivid imagination." Lorna wandered around to the side of the old walls and peered in at the exposed foundation. "Wonder what it would take to restore it."

"Now who has the vivid imagination? I can't even begin to conceive what it would take. And to what purpose? To live way out here, without neighbors, without power? With only a ghost for company?" Amalie laughed. Did her laugh sound a little hollow? "Come on, Let's get back. I'd like a swim before dinner."

****

Later that evening Lorna once again brought up the subject of Ansett Plantation. "You know, something really should be done with it. All that prime land climbing up the mountain. It could be subdivided and sold off in large lots. What a view they'd have. And from the sale of the lots you could easily acquire enough capital to restore the mansion."

"What on earth would I do with an eighteenth century mansion? This little beach house is more than enough for me."

"I don't know yet what you should do with it." Lorna frowned, deep in thought. "Maybe open an inn. Don't you think it a little sad that there is no tourist accommodation on this island? That gorgeous beach and all those great views and no place to stay? I'll bet if you were to build a good inn here the tourists would come in droves."

"Ever the entrepreneur. I believe you would actually do that, Lorna. But I don't think I could. I'm not even sure I'd want tourists coming *in droves*." Amalie thought of Jonathan and the problems they still had to face. Until Jonathan had found peace, no one would be building out on White Wall.

That night Amalie tossed and turned. Her mind kept returning to one of the earlier conversations she'd had with Josephina about the fact that Jonathan must still be here for a reason. That perhaps the events of that night weren't meant to have happened that way. She had suggested that there might have been *some kind of cosmic error* that needed correcting.

And she, Amalie, had shied away from that possibility. She hadn't wanted even to consider it, because if it were true, if they could once again change the events of the past, she would lose Jonathan. He would be of his time. She would have to return to hers. He would have the other Amalie, while she…

What was she thinking? How could she possibly refuse to help him? What kind of love would condemn a man to walking forever as a ghost just so that she could be with him? No. If she loved him, and she knew without a doubt that she did, then she had to help him change the events of the past. Even if that help lost him to her forever.

When Amalie went to Lorna's room three days later, she found her packing.

"I've booked a flight out of St. Luke's tomorrow. I must get back to L.A. One of us has to keep drumming up business."

"So soon? I'll miss you, Lorna."

"I'll be back in three months or so. As I told you, it's neat having a reason to come to the Caribbean regularly. By the way, I won't be here for dinner tonight."

"Oh?"

"I'm having dinner with Edward Sloan."

"Josephina's solicitor?"

"The same."

"Where will you be having dinner? There's no restaurant on St Clement's."

"No. That's why I'm packing now. We're having dinner on St. Luke's. Edward is flying me over in his plane this afternoon."

Amalie looked at Lorna in astonishment. "His plane? When...how..."

A self-satisfied look crossed Lorna's face. "It isn't every day I meet a good looking, intelligent, professional man, who is taller than I am and flies his own plane. I couldn't pass that up."

Amalie laughed. "You're incorrigible."

"Let us say, rather, that I don't let opportunities slip through my fingers. And speaking of opportunities, do you have that surveyor's plot that Edward gave you of Ansett Plantation?"

"Yes, why?"

"Do you mind if I take it with me? I'll bring it back when I come in March."

"I guess not. But whatever for?"

"I have a thought or two. We'll talk about it the next time I'm here."

The house seemed very empty after Lorna left late that afternoon. Amalie wandered through the rooms thinking about Josephina and the hours they'd spent together. She smiled as her eyes struck the cribbage board. She guessed she'd have to teach Jonathan how to play cribbage. Maybe then she'd win.

She heard pots and pans rattling. Who was in the kitchen? She opened the door to find Elvirna in a cloud of pastry flour. "What are you doing here?"

"I makin' brown betty for dessert tonight. I makes it with guavas."

"No. I meant, what are you doing here? You don't need to work. Josephina left you enough so that you never need to work again."

"You crazy? This is my kitchen. I cooks in it. You Miss Josephina's cousin. You lives here. I cooks for you. What else I do with my time?"

"Oh, Elvirna!" Amalie threw her arms around the elderly black woman who had looked after her cousin for more than forty years and was now determined to look after her. "I'm so glad you're back."

"I never left. Jes took a few days off. You be pleased to know my Andrew done got his eyes operated."

"Already?"

"Been three weeks. Had to do it quick before he lose he nerve."

"And?"

"He say he see like when he were a young man."

"That's wonderful, Elvirna."

That night Amalie slept deeply and dreamlessly. She had made the decision to help Jonathan, whatever the personal cost.

CHAPTER 10

The next afternoon, as she lay on the beach in the sun after her swim, Amalie turned her mind to a problem she hadn't discussed with Jonathan. The first time she went back with him to that earlier time, she had coexisted with the other Amalie, one with her, yet not one with her. Her own mind had always operated separately. In a sense she'd been an observer. Oh, not when it came to feelings. Particularly when she was with Jonathan, she was as and with the first Amalie. But at all other times, in some corner of her mind she retained her awareness of self. She allowed her ancestor full control over all actions. She'd never tried to direct or even gently to nudge her in one direction or another.

But things were different the second time. She'd wanted to change the past and to do so she had occupied that other Amalie's mind as well as her body. She wasn't sure how she did that. But she had willed it and it had happened. And the results had been disastrous.

This time she and her ancestor were going to have to act together. If they struggled with each other for control, all could be lost. The consequences would be horrendous. She shuddered as she remembered Amalie losing her mind on that first occasion, when her ancestor had been directing all their actions. And her violent death on the replay, when Amalie of the twenty-first century had made all the decisions. If the events of the past were ever to be changed for the better, they would have to act in agreement with one another. In unison, with one mind. Could they do that? They had to, if they were to prevent the repetition of the mistakes of the past.

And if they succeeded? Could she safely extract herself, find her way back to her own time?

On the other hand, if they were successful in changing what happen on that night once again, this time preventing the murders, would she even want to separate herself from that other Amalie? She could just stay there, being Amalie, loving Jonathan, being loved by Jonathan. She could live out her life in the nineteenth century.

By inhabiting another woman's body, another woman's soul? No. Amalie wasn't quite sure of the meanings of 'moral' and 'ethical', but somehow taking over another woman's life didn't seem either. She would have to find a way back to her own life, her own time. And she would lose Jonathan forever. But then he had never really been hers. He loved her as Amalie, his Amalie who died long ago.

Amalie picked up her towel and trudged back to the beach house.

The future would tell. They would try once again, only this time they would not be impotent puppets. They would act. They would all, she, the first Amalie, Jonathan and Samuel, act together.

That evening when he came to her room, she said, "We're going back."

"Oh?"

"Yes. We must. But there are two problems I haven't yet figured out how to tackle."

"Only two?" he smiled.

"First we have to figure out how to get this key, the key to Benstone's safe, back to the past with us."

"Where did you get that?"

"It was in the showcase at the museum. If we take it back with us we won't have to steal it from Benstone this time. But I can't carry it. I always arrive dressed as the other Amalie. I don't seem to be able to take anything from the present with me."

"But I can. I can carry it in my pocket. My clothing never changes between here and there. One of the minor conveniences of ghost hood. What was the second problem?"

"I always remember the now, my time in the present, when I'm there in the past. I'll remember what is coming in your time. The events of that last night. The night you and Amalie were murdered. But you don't. You never see what's going to happen to you."

"That's right."

"Then somehow we must make you do exactly as I ask when the critical time comes. And I don't for one moment think that nineteenth century gentlemen are accustomed to taking orders from young girls. Even when they're betrothed to them."

Jonathan laughed. "You'll just have to be persuasive. Both in this time and in my own, my Amalie has ever been the master, or should I say mistress, of gentle persuasion."

Amalie thought persuasion seemed a problematic solution, but it was all they had. She just hoped that when the time came, Jonathan would believe her and do what was necessary.

"When do you want to try this?"

"Soon. Before I lose my nerve."

"I'll meet you at Evans Plantation tomorrow morning."

****

Amalie thought she was prepared this time for the transition from present to past. She remembered how frightening it had been on both previous occasions and had braced herself for another terrifying experience. She buried her face against Jonathan's chest as they stepped through the portal. To her surprise, without any seeming gap in time, she found herself whirling in Jonathan's arms to music, to a waltz, the wicked new dance only recently imported to the colonies from Europe. They were on the terrace of the governor's mansion. Other couples swirled around them. The women were all dressed in satins and laces, their full skirts swaying as they moved to the music of a small string orchestra playing on the balcony above.

209

The music ended and Jonathan escorted her back to the table where her father sat in conversation with Edward Benstone, the new Administrator, in whose honor this welcoming ball had been organized.

"Allow me to present my daughter, Amalie and her affianced, Jonathan Evans."

"An honor. I've been hearing about your experimental crops, Evans. Odd that you should be so willing to do away with sugar cane. It has brought the West Indies wealth beyond belief for the last hundred years. I'd like to hear your reasoning some time."

"I should be happy to share my opinions with you at length, but the long and short of it is that I believe the days of slavery are numbered. And when the day comes that planters have to hire their workers, those who wish to survive had better be planting something other than sugar cane. The harvesting and processing of cane is brutal. Few men, given a choice, would ever work in a boiling house."

"Hmm. A curious opinion, to say the least. Don't be so quick to write off slavery. I know our present Parliament has outlawed the transporting of slaves, the slave trade, but freeing all the slaves? That won't happen soon, if ever. Governments change. And with them policies change." Benstone's eyes fell on Amalie. "But enough about politics. May I have a dance with your charming daughter?" he asked Emile Ansett.

210

"Of course."

Bowing briefly to Jonathan, Benstone took Amalie's arm and led her to the dance floor. In moments she found herself in an unyielding embrace, pressed uncomfortably close to the overpowering form of the Administrator. She had the brief thought that dancing with him was a bit like a battle, one she wasn't winning. She just wanted the music to end so that she could escape to Jonathan's arms. How could anyone turn a simple turnabout the dance floor into such a struggle for dominance?

Finally the music ended and Benstone accompanied her back to her father and Jonathan, whose face was thunderous. He took her hand and said, "I believe Amalie needs a bit of fresh air. Please excuse us."

Her father nodded his consent.

Benstone glanced in annoyance at Jonathan before turning his attention back to Amalie. "Of course. I look forward to seeing you soon again, Mistress Ansett."

Once in the garden, removed from the crowd, Jonathan asked, "What was that about?"

"I'm not sure. He confuses dancing with conquest. I don't think I care much for our new Administrator."

The evening went on too long, but finally they were able to go home. Amalie fell gratefully into bed. What was the date? What month was it? This had been no part of her earlier experiences in the past.

"It's the second. The second of December. And welcome back."

Amalie sat bolt upright in bed. The voice was inside her head. It was the other Amalie.

"How do you know I've been here before? What do you remember of the other times?"

The voice inside her head sounded puzzled. "Nothing. I remember nothing really. Only that I am you and you are me and somehow we are two in one body."

"This time we need to be one. To think as one, to act as one. Do you think we can do that?"

"I do not find myself in conflict with you. It's clear to me that we both love Jonathan. I know that whatever we do will be for the best. Now I'm tired. We must sleep."

The next morning when Amalie awoke she wondered if she had dreamed the conversation with her ancestor.

"No. You weren't dreaming. I am with you."

"Good. Then you must know what I know. Benstone is not to be trusted."

"I hardly need you to tell me that. He's a dreadful man. A bully. After just one dance with him I believe I have his measure."

"He will commit murder unless we stop him."

"Murder? I believe him capable of that. But who? Who does he hate that much?"

"Us, Jonathan, your father, Jonathan's man, Samuel."

"Why? We've done him no harm."

"It's a long story. It involves your father and a business deal he made with Benstone."

"But Benstone has just arrived on the island. We've just met him. How can Father be involved with him in any way?"

There was a confused silence between them. Then Amalie asked, "What year is this?"

"Eighteen hundred and nine. It is the tenth of December, eighteen hundred and nine."

A year. They had returned a full year in advance of the terrible events of December, eighteen hundred and ten. They had a year in which to change the course of history. Amalie's relief was huge.

"We must keep Papa from engaging in any business arrangements with Benstone."

"That will be impossible. Clearly you have no idea how little our opinion will be valued in this."

"Nonetheless we must try."

Jemma opened the door. "You is up early. Expected you to sleep later after the party."

"No. Help me dress, Jemma. I want to talk to Papa before he leaves the house this morning."

213

"You is too late for that. He say somethin' about meetin' with the Administrator. Business of some kind."

Too late. Too late to keep him from signing the incriminating papers. Still, they had months ahead of them. If they acted soon, they could still salvage the situation. First she had to get to Jonathan. Make him understand how perilous their situation was. She'd talk to him when they met at the beach in the afternoon.

****

They lay languidly in each other's arms on the warm sand, surfeited with their lovemaking. He reached down and circled her breast lazily with his tongue. "I love the taste of you after swimming, after sex. Salty and sweet at the same time."

Amalie ran her fingers through his soft thick hair, still damp from the sea and kissed him gently on his neck, his lips. How she loved the feel of him on her, in her.

She sighed. "Jonathan, we need to talk." Her tone was serious.

He sat up abruptly. "Something's wrong?"

"Yes. No. That is something will be wrong if we don't take action."

"What are you talking about?"

"It's Benstone. I'm afraid he is trying to involve my father in some scheme that isn't legal. Something that will cause us all great harm if we cannot prevent it."

214

"Scheme? What kind of scheme? The Administrator just arrived on island."

"I'm almost certain he is trying to involve my father in the transportation of slaves."

"But the slave trade was outlawed by Parliament a year ago."

"Exactly. And the profits to be made from the illicit slave trade are, as a result, huge. Papa has been losing money on the plantation for some time now. He'll see Benstone's offer as a way out."

"If this is true, the results could be very dangerous for your father. For your whole family. But how did you come by this information? I can't believe that your father would confide this sort of thing to you."

"I can't explain how I know this, Jonathan. But I do know it to be true."

"Perhaps I should speak to him. If it is simply a matter of a temporary shortage of funds needed to run the Plantation…"

"No. It's more than that. Ansett Plantation has been losing money for the last several years."

"I told your father that he should diversify his crops. He replied that cane was good enough for his father and his grandfather and that it was good enough for him."

"And now he's desperate. With Mother off in England with Tommy, the bills to be met for Tommy's schooling, and Mother's rather extravagant tastes, I'm afraid Papa has gotten over his head in debt."

"Still, engaging in slave running…are you sure? How do you know this?"

There it was, Amalie thought. How did she know? He would never believe the answer to that. "It's just something I overheard."

"I'll check into it; speak to your father. I can't just ask him outright if he's involved in something illegal, but I'll see what I can find out. Meanwhile, please don't worry about this. I'll take care of it."

"I must get back to the house before I'm missed." As she pulled on her boy's clothing, Amalie looked down at the soft brown pants and loose shirt and confided, "Mother keeps sending me frocks and bonnets and gloves from London. I hate to think what they cost. And truthfully, I'd rather have the freedom of these pants, any day."

Jonathan laughed. "I'd hate to be denied the vision of you in your silken gowns, but if it pleases you, you may spend your life dressed as a boy once we're married. Truth be told," he pulled her toward him and kissed her soundly, "I like you best with no clothes on, just fresh out of the sea."

Amalie came back to the problem of her father. "What's to be done?"

"Leave it to me, love. I'll speak with him tomorrow about it. I'm sure the situation can't be as serious as you paint it."

Amalie knew she would have to seek reinforcements. Jonathan must accept her knowledge of what was to come or they would continually reenact the tragedies of the past.

True to his word, Jonathan arrived at ten the next morning and was closeted with her father in his office for over an hour. When he emerged, smiling, the two men shook hands cordially, and her father said, "I'll see you tomorrow night then. I've invited a number of the other planters and their wives, and of course, the new Administrator."

"I'll look forward to it, sir."

"Ah, here is Amalie. She can show you out."

"What did he say?" Amalie asked, leading Jonathan to the foyer.

"Only that he has been invited to join with the Administrator and several other planters in a business venture. You mustn't worry, love. He didn't specify just what kind of business it was, but after talking with him, I'm sure it was nothing illegal."

Amalie stood in the doorway and watched as Jonathan mounted his stallion and galloped off in the direction of Evans House. What was she to do? How could she make him understand what the future held if they didn't act? He had said persuasion. But what kind of persuasion? He had to be made to believe the unbelievable.

That night there were twenty around the dining table at Ansett Plantation. The women wore a rainbow of silks and satins, their jewels sparkling in the soft glow from a candlelit crystal chandelier and a row of silver candelabra down the center of the table. Amalie had created a floral display of hibiscus, frangipani, poinsettias and gardenias between the candles.

Course after course was presented, first a rich lobster bisque, then a fish course, grouper caught just that afternoon and poached in court bouillon, followed by roast beef and Yorkshire pudding. Wine flowed, a white from Bordeaux with the fish, a Chateau Lafite with the beef. The table was abuzz with conversation and alive with laughter.

Finally, when the cheeses and fruits and sweets had been served, Amalie suggested that the ladies, as was customary, should withdraw and leave the gentlemen to their port and cigars.

As she was closing the dining room doors behind her, she heard a snippet of conversation that gave her pause. She stopped and eavesdropped unashamedly. One of the other planters was asking a question of the Administrator.

"That big, fierce-looking man of yours…what's his name?

"You mean Smithins?"

"Smithins. Unusual about here to have a white servant. Our household servants are all Negros. Slaves. How'd you come by him?"

"I found him in Bristol. Actually I saved him from the hangman's noose. You might say he's…grateful."

"Innocent, was he?"

"I hardly think so. All the more reason for him to be grateful."

The room erupted in laughter.

So Smithins had murdered before.

As she moved away from the doors toward the drawing room, Amalie heard her father say, "Port, gentlemen? Or would you prefer brandy?"

As hostess for her father, Amalie presided over the next two hours as the women chatted about their children, their recent shopping forays to St. Luke's, or a hoped for trip to London. Finally the gentlemen joined them and couples began to say their goodbyes.

When the last carriage drew away Amalie breathed a sigh of relief. She enjoyed the company of their friends and neighbors, but the custom of separating the women and men at the end of formal meals had always irked her. Why should women be banished to the drawing room while the men lingered over their port and told ribald stories? She liked ribald stories as well as the next person.

Jonathan usually repeated them to her the next afternoon anyway. But that wasn't the point. Sometimes she felt she had been born into the wrong century. Or perhaps born the wrong sex.

She smiled. No, not the wrong sex. She and Jonathan fit together too well for that. It was as if they had been made of one piece then pulled apart. Both mentally and physically, they completed each other.

Her mind returned to the problem of getting Jonathan to accept that one part of her he didn't yet know, couldn't be expected to understand. Her knowledge of the future. Soon she would have to deal with that.

Tomorrow. Tomorrow she must talk to Samuel.

The next afternoon Amalie knew Jonathan had business in town. She decided there could be no better time.

Slipping quietly out of the house, she headed for Evans Plantation.

She let herself into the office through the doors from the garden.

"Sorry to interrupt you, Samuel."

It happened exactly as before. He looked at her, stunned, as if he were seeing a ghost. His eyes grew wide and his spectacles fell to the floor unnoticed. "Jumbie," he whispered. "Obeah."

Amalie crossed to him and looked deeply into his eyes. "It's all right, Samuel. I tell you it's all right. I'm here to help." She reached to the floor, retrieved his glasses and gently placed them back on his face.

He searched her eyes for a moment and then answered. "Good."

"I need you, Samuel. You will help me won't you?"

He drew in a quick breath then answered, "Of course I will. But who are you? You are not Amalie. Not the Amalie I know."

"I am the Amalie you know. But I am also another Amalie. One who will live two hundred years from now, in the future. Both of us love Jonathan. We want to stop a terrible thing from happening."

"I've never heard of a jumbie from the future, but I suppose it's possible. Some of our Obeah men and women see the future. Is it like that?"

"Yes, Samuel. It's exactly like that." Amalie pulled a chair close to Jonathan's and began to speak in a calm measured voice. She told him in detail about the events of the night of December tenth, eighteen hundred and ten.

His eyes never left hers as she spoke. When she was still, he asked, "Is this inevitable? Can it be changed?"

"We've already changed it once. I made a second trip to the past, to your time."

"What happened?"

Amalie recounted in full detail the events of their second attempt to change the past.

"So you see, we changed the date of the events and even what happened, but Amalie and Jonathan still died. You escaped that time, to the hills."

Samuel's eyes looked into a distant place. He was lost in thought.

Amalie wondered if he accepted what was, after all, an absurd tale.

He brought himself back to the present. "What do you propose that we do?"

Amalie had not realized until that moment that she had been holding her breath. With a grateful sigh, she said, "I'm not completely sure yet. But whatever else we do, we must convince Jonathan of the danger we face. Of the necessity for action. You believe me. That's a start. You have to help me persuade Jonathan of the truth of my warnings, of my ability to read the future."

"Jonathan has a more open mind than most. After all, we grew up together. From him I learned about Christianity. From me he learned about Obeah. He does not scoff at our beliefs, our way of seeing the world."

"We need to talk to him soon."

"Are you planning to meet him here tomorrow?"

"Yes."

"Then tomorrow it will be. I will think about how to approach this."

As it happened it was two days before Amalie had the opportunity to meet Jonathan with Samuel. Her father had taken a notion to have her beside him as he went into town to get supplies and to visit the Administrator. Then they had been invited to luncheon at one of the neighboring plantations. By the time they got home, it was late afternoon. Too late to meet Jonathan at the beach. Much too late to try to have a serious conversation with him. Ah, well. He would be here for dinner. She could try to prepare him a bit for what he was to hear the next day.

Jonathan was the only dinner guest at her father's table that night. After dinner, Emile Ansett retired to his office as was his custom, leaving Jonathan and Amalie to walk in the garden.

They strolled hand in hand. The moon was full and bright and cast a long rippling silver streak across the dark of the sea. They moved to the small jasmine covered gazebo and sat on a bench. They were not completely out of sight of the house, but the lattice and the thick vine climbing it gave them some privacy. The scent of the jasmine perfumed the air. Jonathan leaned down to kiss her lips, a soft entreating kiss. She returned the kiss with ardor, but pulled back before it could deepen into something more.

"Is there something wrong? Something more than your worries over your father? I can assure you they are unfounded."

"Jonathan, tell me what you understand Obeah to be."

He was silent for a moment. "I first learned of Obeah from Kishima, a slave in our household. You know that my mother died giving birth to me. The only mother I ever knew was Kishima. She was kind and patient and endlessly loving. I cared for her deeply."

"You said she died unexpectedly. What happened to her?"

"She died when I was ten. It was an accident in the boiling house. By all rights she shouldn't have been there. She was a household worker, not a field worker. But the drivers said they needed more help. All the slaves on the plantation were pressed into the work of boiling down the sugar. I had never been allowed in or near the boiling house at that time. I only heard about the accident as whispers from the other household slaves later. The drivers use the whip relentlessly during the boiling down of the cane to keep the workers moving. Kishima was a gentle and obedient soul who had never felt the sting of a whip in her life. When it struck her, she lost her footing and fell into the boiling vat."

Jonathan's voice was flat, devoid of emotion. Somehow his pain was more evident than if he had ranted.

"When my father died I had the boiling house dismantled, brick by brick, stone by stone. I left only the chimney standing. It looks like a church tower. I left it standing in her memory."

"I don't know how you survived such a childhood."

"It was from Kishima that I first heard the word Obeah. There were nights when she would steal away to Obeah ceremonies. About four times a year they happened. She always told me when she would be gone for a few hours and she made sure that another of the household slaves stayed with me until she returned. I believe she was one of the high priestesses. I don't know remember exactly about the timing, but I think the important meetings were linked to changes of season and phases of the moon."

"Did she tell you much about Obeah?"

"Only to say it was their religion. The religion they had brought with them from Africa. I thought I knew what that meant. After all, we were Catholics of a sort. My father didn't pay much attention to religion, but he went to Mass on high holy days, and he wanted the priest with him when he died."

"But I've been told Obeah ceremonies involve sacrifice," Amalie said. "A pig or a goat or a rooster. That in the old days in Africa, it used to involve human sacrifice."

"Does Christianity not involve sacrifice? What is Easter all about? What is communion about, but the remembrance of sacrifice? "Jonathan continued. "And then Samuel came into my life. Samuel has powers. He sees things others of us do not. If he were not my friend and the manager of my plantation, I believe he would be an Obeah priest. We've often talked about myth and religion and how one man's faith is another man's superstition."

"Did you ever discuss this with your tutor? You said he was a Jesuit."

"Brother Xavier was always open to such conversations. He has great faith but an amazingly curious mind. Other than Samuel's, I value his opinion more of that than any living man. He found Obeah interesting, and once I think he even saw part of an Obeah ceremony."

"You have been fortunate in those surrounding you."

"I know, but never so fortunate as when you came into my life."
He smiled, remembering. "You were still a child."

"I was fourteen. Some women are married at fourteen."

"You were delicious. I'll never forget my first sight of you. You
were racing your mare along the beach. Your skirts were flying and
your legs were exposed to above your knees. And your hair was all
loose and uncombed and windblown. And my heart stopped. I
believe I have loved you from that moment. I told myself it was
absurd. There was a six year difference in our ages. You were still a
child. But it did no good. I wanted you."

"You never said anything. We met at dinners and at parties, and
on the beach, and you never said anything."

"I was waiting for you to grow up. It was my firm plan to ask
your father for your hand on the day you were eighteen."

"I moved that along, didn't I? Two years later, the day after my
sixteenth birthday." Amalie gave a low seductive laugh. "I waited
quite deliberately for you that day down on the beach."

"How could I forget? You were standing there, so close I could
smell the scent of your hair, feel the warmth of your skin. It was
driving me to distraction. Not touching you was one of the hardest
things I've ever done in my life. Then you said, 'race you' and
started pulling off your clothes. I just stood there, in shock,
immobile."

"Not for long. I seem to recall you divested yourself of clothing pretty rapidly."

"We enjoyed our first kiss, out there in the sea. And I fully meant it to stop there."

Amalie laughed. "I didn't. I came to the beach that day determined to seduce you, to break though that steely reserve once and for all. I wanted you, Jonathan. I wanted you when I first saw you. I still want you." She slid over him, straddling his lap and reached up to kiss him, her tongue entwining with his as his arms came around her, his hands cupping her buttocks. Her hands roamed his body and found their way to his groin. He was rock hard.

Without words she unbuttoned his trousers, lifted her skirts and fitted herself onto his shaft. He groaned. She took him deeply into her and started moving. She bit her lips to keep from crying out as he reached between her legs to rub. She pushed against his hand, twisting, rocking, in frenzy. At the last moment he tried to withdraw, but she fastened her legs tight around him. He exploded deep into her as she climaxed and fell limp against him.

When they could once again breathe, Jonathan placed his hand gently under her chin and raised her face so that she had to look into his eyes. "Amalie, I've explained why I must withdraw at the end. It will not do for you to become pregnant while we're unwed."

"And I've told you that I cannot do that. I want your seed inside me. If I find I'm with child, we'll marry quickly and quietly. Do you suppose we would be the first ever to do so?"

"What am I to do with you, Amalie?"

"Keep doing what you just did." Amalie started to straighten and rearrange her clothing and smooth her tangled hair.

He adjusted his own clothes and shook his head. "I've never understood how you could have grown up so free and uninhibited."

"I suppose it had to do with a mother who was never there and a father who was just too busy to notice. No one ever really stopped me from doing anything I chose to do."

"Most young women of your age would faint at the mere mention of sex. You came to me a virgin and virtually forced yourself on me."

"Forced myself on you indeed! You were more than willing, as I recall."

"How could I not have been? I had dreamt of you night after night for two years and there you were before me, naked as a Jay bird, dripping from the sea, arms about my neck, pressing yourself against me. It would have taken a stronger man than I to resist." He laughed. "At sixteen, and a virgin, how could you have known so much about seduction?"

"You forget I grew up virtually motherless on a working plantation. I saw my father's stallion mount my mare when I was just twelve. I thought it was rather magnificent. Later I watched my mare drop her foal. I made the necessary connections."

"Are you comparing me to a stallion?"

Amalie stood back and gazed pointedly at his crotch. "Hmm. Not at the moment."

Jonathan's laugh boomed out.

Emile Ansett emerged from the garden. "I thought I might find you here. It's a beautiful spot at the full moon isn't it? What were you laughing at?"

"Your daughter, sir. She was telling me a story about your stables."

The three walked slowly back to the house. Jonathan decorously kissed Amalie's hand and bid her good night. Then he turned to her father. "Could we speak privately for a moment?"

"Of course. Come into the parlor. Would you like a brandy?"

****

When they were seated, snifters in hand Jonathan broached once again the subject of his betrothal to Amalie and of their already long wait.

"I think it is time we wed, sir. Evans Plantation is doing very well. We've had a profitable year. I can support Amalie in the style to which she is accustomed. And to be frank, sir, I'd like to start a family. My home has been too long without a woman's touch."

Emile Ansett looked down in thought. "I understand your impatience, my boy. But Amalie's mother would raise bloody hell if her only daughter were to be married in her absence. She has plans for a big wedding."

"But when can we expect her back on Island? She's been in London for years now."

"I wish I knew. Her letters are infrequent. She's enjoying London society and she seems in no hurry to return to our little outpost of the Empire."

Jonathan sighed. "I suppose we can wait a bit longer. But will you at least try to get some idea of when she intends to return?"

"I can try. I'll send a letter by the next post telling her of your request to set a date. She does approve of your suit, you know."

Jonathan nodded. He supposed with that he would have to be satisfied.

CHAPTER 11

The next afternoon Amalie managed to find Jonathan and Samuel together in the office at Evans House.

"I'll be with you in just a moment, Amalie." Jonathan turned back to Samuel. "So you think there might be a good market for tobacco?"

"It's is widely used both in Europe and America. I think we need to investigate further, but it's being grown successfully on other islands."

"Good. Let's do so." He turned smiling to Amalie and held out his hand "Shall we go for a swim?"

"Actually, no. We need to talk, the three of us." Amalie sat down.

"The three of us?" Jonathan gave a puzzled frown, but sat down also, looking from Amalie to Samuel, and back to Amalie. "About what?"

"First I remind you of what you told me about Obeah last night. You must keep an open mind. And you must believe what I tell you."

"You have never lied to me, Amalie. Why should I not believe you whatever you say?"

Samuel broke in. "You may have difficulty with what Amalie is about to say. It defies everything you've been brought up to believe."

A tense silence followed. Jonathan looked from one to the other of the two people he loved and respected more than anyone in the world. "What is it?"

Amalie took a deep breath and plunged in. "I know the future, Jonathan. I more than know it. I have lived in it."

Jonathan frowned. "Samuel has always had some gift for prophesy. Are you telling me you have the same gift?"

Samuel broke in. "No, Jonathan. I sometimes have a glimmer of what is to come. Amalie knows without question. She knows because she is from the future."

"What…this is some kind of jest you're having with me, surely?"

"No, Jonathan." Samuel shook his head. "No jest. Your bride to be, Amalie Ansett, lives both now and two hundred years in the future and I assure you what she is about to tell you is fact. It is history yet to happen. Listen to her with an open mind."

Numb with shock, Jonathan sat back and nodded.

Encouraged, Amalie began her story, telling him of her encounter with his ghost in the twenty-first century. Jonathan's eyes widened as she talked about meeting him, falling in love with him, and traveling back with him to his own time where she became one with the Amalie of his time.

When she paused, looking at him for some response, he merely shook his head. "What can I say? It's beyond belief. You are telling me that at this moment there are two of you inhabiting one body and that one of those entities is from the future?"

"That's about it."

Jonathan looked at Samuel. Samuel nodded.

"Why? Assuming that such things were possible, why would my spirit still be on earth two hundred years from now? And why would the two of us return to the past?"

Amalie used Josephina's words. "We think there may have been some cosmic error. We believe that the events of that night should never have happened and your ghost will wander until that error is corrected. When you found me in the future, I became the catalyst for change."

"You said the events of that night. What night? What events?"

Amalie took a deep breath and told Jonathan exactly what happened on the night of December tenth, eighteen hundred and ten.

Jonathan was silent for a long time after she finished. Finally he spoke softly. "So, according to you, we will all die at the hands of the Administrator and his henchman more or less a year from now?"

"Yes. No. Not exactly. You see we came back again."

"Came back again." Jonathan spoke in a monotone.

Amalie proceeded to recount the events of their disastrous second voyage to the past.

233

Jonathan put his head in his hands then looked at Samuel. "You believe this?"

"I more than believe. I know it to be true. I see Obeah in Amalie. As she tells her story I see flashes of the events in my mind. I was there. I was there both times."

Amalie continued, "Don't you see, Jonathan? If we changed history once we can change it again. This is our third chance and I have a terrible feeling it's our last."

Jonathan shook his head. "It's too much to absorb. If there were any tangible evidence, anything I could grasp of reality…"

Suddenly Amalie smiled. "Those brown pants of yours. The ones you wear when you're working in the fields or riding…"

"What about them?"

"Go get them."

Samuel darted off and came back moments later holding the garment.

"These are what you were wearing the night you were murdered. These are the only pants I have ever seen you wear as a jumbie."

"Go on."

"You remember I struggled with Benstone for the key to the safe on our second trip to the past?"

"Yes, so you said."

"Reach into the pocket."

Jonathan drew in his breath sharply as his fingers encountered metal. He pulled the brass key out of the small pocket the waistline of his pants.

Amalie sat back, relieved. She hadn't been sure until that moment that the key had made the crossing with them intact.

The silence lengthened. Finally Jonathan spoke. "What are we to do?"

"I think the secret to outwitting Benstone lies in his safe. If he tricked my father into this nefarious business, I should imagine he has done the same with a number of the other plantation owners. Everyone has felt the pinch since the European market turned to beets for their sugar. Every plantation owner is struggling."

"Except for us," Samuel said. "Our success with alternate crops is a thorn in the Administrator's side. What we can do, others can emulate. A planter who is doing well would not be easy prey. That may be one reason for his intense dislike of Jonathan."

"Just so." Amalie turned to Jonathan. "We need to acquire the contents of that safe and if they are as incriminating as I think they may be, we need to place them before the Governor on St. Luke's."

"Sir Anthony Everett? I've heard he's a good man. Level headed."

"And he'll listen to us. He's my godfather." Amalie smiled.

For the first time that afternoon, Jonathan laughed. "It pays to have friends in high places."

235

Samuel took a small worn leather-covered book off his desk and thumbed through it.

"What's that?"

"Astrological signs, phases of the moon, positions of the stars at different times of the year. We never plant a new crop without consulting it."

Jonathan's eyebrows went up. "Is that a fact?"

"I saw no need to burden you with it."

"Is it going to help us in this?"

"It is. There will be a new moon on December thirty-first."

"New Year's Eve. There will be parties and reveling all over the island."

"Exactly." Samuel tapped the little book. "But more importantly for our purposes, that new moon heralds one of the most important Obeah ceremonies of the year. Every slave who can steal away after midnight will be up on Mt. Zingara that night for that highest of our holy traditions."

"How can that help us?"

"I think it can help us escape. Stealing the contents of that safe may not be difficult, but getting off this island with them could be. Benstone's not stupid. He may well suspect who's behind the theft, and even if he doesn't, he can commandeer any of the ships in the harbor to give chase. He has troops at his disposal. Slipping through the cracks will require cunning." Samuel looked long at Amalie. "And some degree of fortitude."

Amalie knew he was warning her. She wasn't sure exactly about what, but she knew the warning was not a casual one. "I understand."

Jonathan said, "I think we will leave the planning to you Samuel. Tell us what you want us to do and we'll do it."

"For the moment," Samuel said, "it is important that you keep up every appearance of going about your normal lives. This is the season of parties and dances. Go to them all. Disarm the Administrator with your charm, Amalie. Be the affable planter, Jonathan. And for God's sake get off your platform about the emancipation of the slaves. I know how you feel about that, but for the next fifteen days, swallow your feelings. We must not arouse any suspicion."

"Agreed."

Amalie stood. "I'd best be getting home. I don't want Papa to note my absence. Thank you, Samuel. Thank you for everything." She walked over to where the slight black man with the huge intelligence sat at his desk and kissed him on his cheek.

Jonathan burst out laughing. "I've never seen a black man blush before." He swatted Amalie on her behind. "Off with you, before I decide to take my share of the kisses. And that would surely make you late."

On the beach the next afternoon Amalie confided a worry to Jonathan. "It's that man, Smithins. He's big and strong as an ox and has killed before. He'll be guarding the Governor's Mansion whether Benstone is there or not. Be sure to warn Samuel of that as he is drawing up our plans."

"I will. Now about your bestowing your affections on other men..."

"Other men?"

"Samuel. Brazen hussy. You kissed him right in front of me."

"So I did. Jonathan has it never occurred to you that he may be lonely?"

"Lonely? He has me for company."

"I see. And you think he has no need for anyone else, a woman perhaps?"

"A...good God. I've never thought about Samuel in that light."

"The very gifts you gave him, his freedom and his education, isolate him. He has no one except you, and more recently, me. And he has that incredible mind. Where would he ever find a suitable mate?"

"I must say I've never considered it before from his viewpoint. I shall have to see who I can find."

"Jonathan you can't just choose a woman for him. It's not like a puppy. That's something a man must do for himself."

"What do you suggest, then?"

"Perhaps, when this is all over, you might travel to Martinique, just the two of you. Find some crop you want to investigate. I've heard tell the quadroons there are very beautiful and that many are quite well educated. The French have a more relaxed view of race than we English seem to be able to manage. It might come to nothing, but it's worth a try."

Jonathan laughed. "Conniving little witch. Planning everyone else's lives. I shall have to keep you endlessly with child just to keep you busy, to give you enough fodder for that fertile imagination."

"Promises, promises."

There were parties every night. Dinners, dances, soirees, musicales. The island turned itself out in all its holiday splendor. Amalie danced until her feet ached and smiled until her cheeks hurt. She was charming to portly grey haired planters and to dimpled young officers and she was particularly attentive to the Administrator.

Jonathan managed to avoid talking about the superiority of pineapples as an alternative crop to sugar cane and never once mentioned how abhorrent he found the practice of slavery.

On the thirtieth of December they met to review their final plans.

Samuel spoke. "It is agreed then? Jonathan will stand guard while I obtain the papers from the safe. You, Amalie, will remain behind the Anglican Church with our horses. Once I have the documents we must be away swiftly. Time is of the essence. The more space we can put between ourselves and Benstone the easier it will be. When he realizes the theft has taken place, we'll want him to think the culprit is escaping via the harbor. That would be the most natural escape route. We will, of course, be going in the opposite direction, up the slopes of Mt. Zingara."

"But Smithins?"

"I hear tell that he was complaining to some of the off duty officers about having to guard the Governor's mansion every night while the Administrator is out partying. Five of those officers plan to have their own celebration in Smithins' quarters tomorrow night after the Administrator leaves for the evening. I have arranged for several very special bottles of wine to be delivered to them, along with some kidney pies with an unusual extra ingredient. As a New Year's gift from the Administrator."

"Poison?"

"No. Just enough sleeping draught to keep them all unconscious for several hours."

"Pity. I should really like to see Smithins dead." Amalie gave a twisted smile.

"We'll leave him to the hangman."

Just before eleven on New Year's Eve they set out. All three were dressed in black. Amalie and Jonathan had used lamp black on their faces and hands and Amalie had braided her hair tightly so that no tendril could escape to expose her, and then tied a dark scarf over it. Her hair around her face, like her skin, had been blackened. Jonathan had done the same, as Samuel had instructed. The night was dense and dark, almost starless. Wisps of clouds scurried across the pallid silver streak that was the new moon. Their horses pawed in the darkness, picking up the nervousness of their riders.

Silently they threaded their way through town, using the dark back alleys, stopping and waiting whenever they heard sounds of revelers close by. They reached the Anglican Church just twenty minutes before midnight. The doors stood wide and it was brightly lit. The congregation was singing a familiar hymn. The Watch Night service was underway. They had twenty minutes in which to do what they must and get away. At midnight the bells would ring in the New Year and worshipers would pour out to the streets, to stroll, or to climb into their carriages or onto their horses and make their way home, creating confusion and a diversion should the trio need one.

They stopped in the shadows behind the church. Amalie took the three horses' leads and the two men moved as silently as the shadows they resembled, toward the Governor's mansion.

While Jonathan monitored the entrance Samuel went around to the side and let himself silently into the library. The key fit and the safe swung open noiselessly. Without looking to see what he was taking, Samuel scooped the entire contents into his satchel and was

241

turning to leave when the inside door crashed open and the huge figure of Smithins stood there swaying drunkenly, holding an oil lamp high.

"What the…"

The thought was never completed as Jonathan brought a chair down across the man's head.

"Let's get out of here."

The two men ran as they heard shouting behind them. "Smithins? Smithins? What the hell?"

Glancing back, Jonathan saw a soldier outlined in the entrance way, shouting, "Stop, thief! Robbery! Stop them!" He rushed out the door and towards the barracks to get reinforcements.

Jonathan and Samuel slid behind the church just as the bells began to ring from every church in the town. People flooded into the streets.

The three mounted their steeds and once again moved as silently as possible through the dark back streets until they reached the outskirts of town. They had just begun to relax when they came face to face with a carriage full of drunken revelers on their way back to town.

"Hey!" The driver called to them. "What you doin' all blacked up like that. Up to no good I'll be bound!"

They gave their horses their heads. They rode like the wind for the better part of an hour until they came to the end of the zigzagging track up the side of Mt. Zingara.

Samuel dismounted and indicated the others should do the same. "That was an unfortunate encounter. If he tells anyone what he saw, the militia will be looking for us up here, rather than down at the harbor."

"Perhaps he'll have forgotten by the time he gets into town. He didn't sound particularly sober." Jonathan looked around him. "What now? We've come as far as our horses can take us."

"From here on, we're on foot. First we must unsaddle our horses and put their saddles over here in this ditch. I'll cover them with underbrush."

Amalie started to do as instructed, but said, "Why…?"

"Because we've been seen on the way here. They may have been able to identify us by our mounts. They're well-known on the island. If so, Benstone will check at Ansett and Evans Plantations. If our horses are where they belong, unsaddled, in their stalls, he may inquire no further."

"Home, Jesse." He slapped his horse gently on its flanks and it headed at a brisk pace down the slope.

Jonathan and Amalie followed suit. They watched as Molly and Adonis disappeared down the track.

"Now what?"

243

"Now you put these on." Samuel handed them each a long white hooded robe, and donned one himself. "From this moment, keep your eyes down and your head covered. Do exactly as I say. Do not speak. Do not utter a sound. Your lives depend on it."

Amalie saw lights flickering through the trees ahead of them. As the three came to a stop, she saw slaves arriving from multiple directions holding candles, all walking slowly, merging into a single line in absolute silence. They were dressed in long white hooded robes of the kind Samuel had provided for them. Samuel lit three candles, handed them each one, and motioned they should take their places in the procession, Jonathan first, Amalie in the middle, Samuel last. They walked ever upward in the eerie quiet of the forest until they reached the very edge of the crater. There below them was a giant natural amphitheater. There seemed to be hundreds already congregated here, all sitting in silence on the inside slopes. As newcomers filed in, they took their places among the others. The masses of candles shed their light on expressionless black faces, male and female, young, middle aged, and old.

Amalie glanced guardedly around her. There seemed to be a pit of some sort down in the center, at the apex of the amphitheater. An altar?

Then she became aware of sound, chanting, so soft at first it was almost sensed rather than heard. It grew in volume and intensity. Rhythmic, strong, primitive. The crowd was pressed tightly together now, shoulders touching shoulders. A solid human wall. As the chanting grew louder that wall began to sway from side to side. Amalie, with Jonathan on one side of her and Samuel on the other, moved with the rest. The chanting was louder now and faster. Sounds repeated endlessly, belonging to no language Amalie had ever heard.

With a suddenness that almost made Amalie cry out, a deep drum sounded from high on the slopes, beating out a complex African rhythm. It was joined by another and another from the back and sides of the hill.

As if in response to some unseen signal, the chanting stopped abruptly. Two figures stepped into the center of the amphitheater, a man and a woman, both dressed in brilliantly colored robes. The air was heavy, the tension tangible. The congregation leaned forward as one, in anticipation.

A third figure appeared at the altar, carrying a live rooster by its feet. The hapless creature was squawking and flapping its wings. The woman at the altar took a large knife from the folds of her gown.

Amalie whispered, "I think I'm going to be sick."

Jonathan hissed, "Don't you dare."

There seemed to be a commotion from the highest point of the amphitheater, behind the last rows of worshipers.

"Move, blast you. I said move! Let me through." The voice was strident, demanding. Benstone pushed his way toward the altar.

245

He was followed at a distance by a handful of reluctant soldiers roused from their drunken slumbers and pressed into service. The Administrator strode down the side of the amphitheater toward the altar, pushing people roughly out of his way as he made his way forward. The soldiers looked fearfully around them, at the sea of black faces, at the altar, at the sacrificial rooster, and, as one, slowed their advance and began edging carefully back up the slope and away from the scene.

Benstone was unaware that he was alone as he approached the inner circle.

He stepped in front of the altar turned to address the crowd. "I'm sure you know that to assemble in this way is unlawful. But I am merciful and will neither say nor do anything about it. You have only to help me find three escaped criminals. I know they are somewhere on this mountain. I offer freedom to the man who finds and brings them to me."

There was absolute silence. No man moved.

"Are you deaf? You are slaves, are you not? I said I will free the man who brings me Jonathan Evans and the slave called Samuel and the whore who travels with them."

Amalie swallowed her instinctive gasp. How had he discovered their identities so quickly? The people in the cart must have recognized them by their horses. Samuel had been afraid of that.

The entire assemblage seemed frozen in the moment. Every eye was on the Administrator.

The priest who had brought out the sacrificial rooster raised it high and released it. It half flew, half ran into the crowd. Then he turned toward the Administrator. The mass of white robed figures rose as one and began to chant as they pressed toward the altar.

"I think we will leave now," Samuel murmured. Twenty minutes later they were deep in the cool dark of the rainforest.

There, Amalie threw up the remains of her supper. When Jonathan wiped her face with his handkerchief dampened from their water jug, she asked, "What will happen to him?"

Samuel answered, "You don't want to know." Then he looked around. "I think we're safe for the moment, but we can't remain here. We can't be certain those soldiers won't suffer an attack of conscience and come looking for us. We'll have to climb the wall on the other side of the crater and make our way down to the shoreline."

"Then what?"

"I have the ketch hidden in the cove. We'll sail for St. Luke's. With the wind filling the mizzen mast sail, and a little help with the oars, we should make it by morning."

CHAPTER 12

Anthony Everett was just finishing his morning tea when the butler came to him and said, "Beg pardon, Sir Anthony, but there are three *persons* who say they must see you. I have asked them to wait in the hall."

"Persons?"

"I'm afraid they look quite…dirty. At least two of them do. The other seems to be dark naturally."

The Governor General of the Windward Islands frowned. "Did they state their business?"

"One of them, a young boy, said that he was your…goddaughter? Although how that could be possible…"

"Amalie?" The Governor laughed. "With Amalie, anything is possible." He threw down his white linen serviette and strode into the hall. "Amalie. My God, look at you. You're filthy. What happened? How did you get here? And who are these men with you?"

"Good morning, Uncle Anthony. This is my fiancé, Jonathan Evans, and this is Samuel, his plantation manager. We've…"

248

"No. Stop. Before we do anything else, go get cleaned up. What is that black stuff all over your face and hands? It's even in your hair, Amalie. Martha will kill me if I let you anywhere near her drawing room in your present state. Meyers, take them all upstairs and order baths. Find the gentlemen some clean clothes and ask my wife to find something suitable for Mistress Ansett."

Amalie smiled. "Thank you, Uncle Anthony. I knew you would help us."

"Of course, my dear. Have you breakfasted? No. Of course not. I'll have a full morning tea brought to you. We'll reconvene in the library in an hour and a half. Then you can tell me what this is all about."

He shook his head as the three left following the butler.

"Extraordinary."

****

Later that morning, considerably cleaner but still weary from a night without sleep, the three sat in chairs arranged in front of the Governor's desk.

"Are you all right, Amalie? What in God's name caused this precipitous flight in the middle of the night? I assume you must have been in some danger to have resorted to such extreme measures."

"We were, indeed, in grave danger, Uncle Anthony."

"Would you care to explain?"

249

"We were being pursued by the Administrator and a band of soldiers. If he had caught us he would have killed us. We escaped by using an Obeah ceremony as a diversion. Then we climbed down Mt. Zingara to where Samuel had hidden a boat, and here we are." Amalie sat back as if everything necessary had been said. How could she possibly tell her godfather that they were escaping from a murder that would happen a year from now if they hadn't acted?

"Benstone. I worried about his appointment when it was made. But I don't understand, my dear. Why was he pursuing you?"

Samuel interjected. "I think, my Lord, if you examine the papers in this satchel, you may begin to see what this is all about."

The Governor took the proffered bag and emptied its contents out on his desk. Among numerous papers were several large bundles of cash.

"Where did you get all this?"

Jonathan spoke. "From the safe in the Governor's Mansion. To put it bluntly, we burgled it last night. We didn't realize there was cash in there as well. We were in a hurry. Samuel just scooped it all into the satchel. We haven't opened it until now. We had our hands rather full, sir."

Amalie spoke again. "Benstone has been coercing planters to invest in illicit slave running."

"That's an offense punishable by confiscation of properly and imprisonment. Surely the planters on St. Clement's would not have chanced that."

"They've all been having problems lately and, well, they're looking for help from whatever quarter they can get it."

The governor nodded. "Here, too. The island economies are going to have to adjust to new realities and planters are a conservative lot. They don't take easily to change. Except for you, Evans. I've heard good things about you and your experimental crops."

"Thank you, sir."

"Now, if I'm to make any sense of this mess you have dumped in my lap, you're going to have to give me time to sort through all these papers. Perhaps you might like to get a little rest while I do that."

Gratefully, they all retired to rooms that had been made up for them. Amalie thought briefly of trying to find where they had put Jonathan, but she fell asleep contemplating the problem.

It was late in the afternoon when they met again in the library.

"I have some interesting news for you." The Governor picked up a small black notebook and showed it to them. "Benstone was a methodical man. He kept meticulous track of every transaction. It's all in here. Names, dates, amounts. Enough to put him in prison for a very long time if we ever catch up with him."

Samuel spoke. "I don't think prison is an option, my Lord. I suspect he has already paid for his crimes."

251

"Be that as it may, he developed a very interesting way of siphoning money out of the local economy. From men who had little money to spare and were desperate enough to believe his lies."

"They were investing in slaving ships, weren't they?" Jonathan asked.

"They certainly thought they were. That's what he told them. That's what the papers they all signed indicated."

"But…"Amalie looked at her Godfather, puzzled.

"The money they invested never left the island. It was all still in Benstone's safe. He would periodically pay someone their share of the *profits* then persuade them to reinvest it or to invest even more. Eventually he would have told them the ship they invested in was sunk in a storm or caught by a British naval vessel and their money was unfortunately lost. But not before the last penny had been extracted from the last planter. Then I expect he planned to take off to greener pastures."

Jonathan mused, "Meanwhile, if any of them wanted out, he had the incriminating papers with which to threaten them. It's an ingenious scheme."

"Just so. What I don't understand is how you caught this so soon. He had only just begun. He had taken a number of small payments from planters, but clearly he planned to take much more. He could have amassed a small fortune in a year or so. What led you to suspect him?"

252

"It was my father," Amalie said. "He was conscience ridden. I knew something was wrong."

"Good girl. Well, the planters have broken no actual laws. They're victims rather than outlaws. Somehow I'll get the money back to them, but I think with strings attached." He smiled. "Perhaps it could be offered to them as money with which to plant alternative crops."

Jonathan burst out laughing. "Isn't that coercion, Sir Anthony?"

"Let us, rather, say incentive."

"It's approaching dinner time." The Governor looked at Samuel. "You will be the first man of color ever to sit at my table. I want you to know you are welcome here."

"Thank you, sir."

"Not at all. You saved my goddaughter's life. You are a brave man and a resourceful one."

The Governor turned his attention to Jonathan and cleared his throat. "You have been betrothed to my goddaughter for a very long time."

"It seems like an eternity, sir."

"What's keeping you from the altar?"

"Her mother. Her mother is in London and insists that we await her return."

"Sarah Ansett isn't going to be returning from London any time soon. She's having the time of her life. She has never been content with the social life of a small island." He turned to Amalie. "Sorry, my dear, but it's true."

"I know, Uncle Anthony. I've always known that my mother and my father weren't well suited."

"So that leaves us with one other problem as I see it."

Amalie frowned. "Problem?"

"I'm shocked, my dear. Shocked beyond belief. You have spent the night, unchaperoned, with two gentlemen. Your reputation will be in tatters."

"But…"

"No buts about it, Amalie. You will have to marry Jonathan Evans immediately, tonight, or you will never be able to hold your head up in polite society again." There was a broad smile on Sir Anthony Everett's face as he spoke these words.

"Oh, Uncle Anthony!" Amalie ran to her godfather and hugged him.

"Most indecorous." He laughed. "Now go find Martha and have her arrange something that will do as a wedding dress. I must call the Bishop."

Jonathan stood and shook the Governor's hand. "Thank you, sir."

****

Amalie Ansett and Jonathan Evans were wed at St. James at ten o'clock that evening, attended only by Sir Anthony Everett, his wife, Martha, and Samuel.

254

The bride wore a full skirted dress of pale blue silk satin trimmed at the neck and at the wrist with cream colored lace. It had been Martha Everett's wedding dress when she had been much younger and much slimmer. Amalie carried a bouquet of island gardenias and their sweet scent filled the air. The church organist had been pressed into service.

Sir Anthony gave the bride away, standing in for her father, and the gold band slipped onto her finger had come from a local goldsmith whose supper had been interrupted by a summons from the Governor.

Samuel served as best man.

When the simple ceremony was over, the bride and groom and the rest of the wedding party moved to the church office to sign the necessary documents.

When it came Samuel's turn to sign as witness, he wrote simply. *Samuel.*

"Oh my, that won't do. You must sign your full name," the priest instructed.

"But that is my full name. It's the only name I've ever been given. Slaves have only one name and when I was freed I still had no other name."

Jonathan's voice came strong and clear. "Your name is Evans. Samuel Evans. What else would it be? You are my brother."

255

The two men stared into each other's eyes. Then Samuel smiled and wrote *Evans* in the record book.

Much later that night, snuggling in her husband's arms in the afterglow of lovemaking, Amalie murmured, "That was a wonderful thing you did for Samuel tonight."

"Giving him a name?"

"No. Giving him a family."

They were silent for a few moments, enjoying the luxury of time.

Amalie said, "You know, this will be the first time we've ever been able to sleep together. To be able to sleep and wake in the morning together."

"Hmm. I wasn't planning on sleep just yet." He nuzzled her neck and placed his hand between her legs. "I hope you weren't. I'm not quite through with you for the evening."

"No?" She wriggled against his touch and slid her own hands down his body to find him once again ready. "I see what you mean. What shall we do about you? It seems you have a problem. You're insatiable. Fortunately for you, you have married the right woman."

She gave a low throaty laugh and slowly fitted herself over and around him, taking him fully into her.

Yes. They were as one person, body and soul.

****

Dawn crept through the window. Amalie turned her head into her pillow. She wasn't ready to wake up yet. Her body was heavy from long love making. Feeling a small aftershock of pleasure and the reawakening of desire, she turned toward her husband. The bed beside her was empty.

She pushed up onto her elbow. At that moment Enrico crowed beneath her balcony.

"No!" The cry held all the anguish of a world lost. "No, no. Not yet."

She wept until there were no tears left. Then numbly she arose and dressed. She would walk on the beach.

She walked blindly, reliving the last days and nights they'd spent together. How could she live without him?

Before this third and last trip to the past, she had determined that she had no right to continue to inhabit her ancestor's body once their mission was accomplished. She had vowed to return to her own time, to leave that other Amalie with her Jonathan.

But she wasn't ready yet. Not yet.

Somehow she got through the next days and weeks. She saw no one. She answered Elvirna's increasingly concerned questions with monosyllabic answers. She tried to eat the food set in front of her, but she had no appetite. Her clothes began to hang on her and her hair, once her glory, was dull and stringy.

She was always chilled. The tropical warmth never seemed to reach her.

The day came when it seemed too much effort to get out of bed. Elvirna came and forced her to get up and helped her to shower and dress. Then she led her to the veranda and put food in front of her, coaxing her to eat.

The doctor came by one day. He listened to her heart, took her blood pressure, and left Elvirna a small vial of pills which Amalie dutifully took whenever Elvirna handed her one. They seemed to make no difference.

It had been a month since her return. Amalie sat on the veranda staring sightlessly out to sea when she heard a familiar voice behind her.

"Good God, Amalie! What have you been doing to yourself? You look like death warmed over."

"Lorna!" Amalie threw herself into her friend's arms and the dam burst. All the sorrow that had been eating at her for the last two months found release. She sobbed helplessly. Then she was hiccupping, gasping for breath.

Lorna unwound Amalie's arms from around her neck and sat her down gently. Then she called to Elvirna to bring them some tea. She sat quietly holding Amalie's hands in her own until the hiccupping stopped and Amalie was breathing more normally.

Elvirna came out on the veranda with a full tray. There were scones and jam and butter as well as a pot of aromatic Earl Grey tea.

"I'm glad you is here. She don't eat, she don't drink, she don't sleep. She jes wastin' away and nothin' I do helps."

"You did the right thing when you called me, Elvirna. I'll take care of her."

"Thank the Lord. Now make she eat somethin'." Elvirna shook her head. "She don't listen to me when I tells she to eat." Elvirna disappeared back indoors, muttering to herself.

"Lorna, I..."

"No. No explanations now. Drink your tea and eat a scone. We'll take a walk on the beach and talk once you've eaten. I'm hungry, too. I've just survived two days of airplane food and those scones of Elvirna's look heavenly." Lorna took one off the plate and slathered it liberally with butter and jam. Amalie sat quietly, her hands clenched.

Lorna frowned, pulled Amalie's hands apart and put the scone in one of them. "Eat." she ordered.

Amalie looked at the scone as if not comprehending what it was or how it got there, but she took a bite then another until it was finished. She licked the crumbs and butter off her fingers.

"Good," Lorna said. "Now drink some tea."

When there was nothing left on the tray, Lorna stood and pulled Amalie to her feet. "Let's go for a walk. I've missed walking on this beach."

They trudged along through the sand in silence for a few moments then Lorna turned toward Amalie.

"Are you going to tell me about it, Amalie? It was a man, wasn't it? I suspected there was a man the last time I was here. Did the bastard leave you?"

Amalie frowned in thought. Jonathan hadn't left her. He loved her. He would never have left her. He was with her in that other earlier time. He wasn't with her here because...

"He's dead," Amalie said, accepting the truth of it for the first time.

She frowned in thought. Jonathan was dead. He had been dead for many years now. Saying the words somehow freed Amalie from the dark place where she'd been living, shattered, since her return from the past. The sorrow was still there, it might be there forever, but it was just sorrow, not despair. The emptiness in her soul lifted ever so slightly.

"I loved him and he loved me, and he's dead. And I've been having trouble trying to live without him. But I think I'm going to be all right now that you're here. Thank you for coming, Lorna."

"Do you want to tell me about it, about him?"

"No, Lorna, I can't. Except that to have loved him and been loved by him was a gift. He's in his grave now and I'm alone. But I will survive. He would expect that of me." As she said the words Amalie knew they were true. Jonathan would have wanted her to survive, to get on with her life.

"Very well. Let's start this survival process by doing something about the way you look. How much weight have you lost?"

Amalie looked down at herself and shook her head. "I haven't felt much like eating."

"Clearly. You've lost at least twenty pounds. Your hair is a mess and your clothes are just hanging on you."

Amalie yawned. "I'm suddenly very sleepy. Would you mind if left you for a little while and took a nap?"

"Not at all. You look like you could use some sleep. I'll be here when you wake up."

****

Lorna had a thousand questions, but she suspected none of them would ever be answered. Clearly, Amalie did not want to talk about it. Very well. She would put a leash on her curiosity. She didn't need to know who or what or when. Although how Amalie could have carried on a love affair on this little island with none the wiser defied imagination. Lorna's main concern must be for Amalie. Whoever he was, his death had hit Amalie hard. Lorna decided that to pull Amalie out of her depression, drastic measures were needed.

She took out her cell phone.

261

"Edward? It's Lorna. I'm here on St. Clement's…Yes it was an unexpected trip…Amalie hasn't been well and she has such a look of fragility about her that I'm really worried."

"Yes, yes, the doctor has seen her. He's given her anti-depressants. But she's not eating, and I suspect she's not sleeping."

"That's why I called. I need to get Amalie away for a few days. I thought maybe a spa on St. Luke's? You could? Oh that would be darling of you. Yes, three o'clock this afternoon will be fine. We'll be ready. It will be good to see you."

When Amalie awoke from her nap Lorna had her plans all made.

"We're going over to St. Luke's for a few days and get the works. I've signed us into a resort there. We're going to get massages and facials and get our hair done. And while we're at it, we'll shop for some new clothes. You must have dropped at least two sizes. I hope you'll gain some of it back, but meanwhile we can't have you going around with tops two sizes too large and pants that are falling off you. Go get packed."

Confused, Amalie said, "But there are no more flights out today, Lorna."

"Edward is flying us there. He'll stay over and have dinner with us if you don't mind."

For the first time in weeks, Amalie smiled. "It's good to have you here Lorna."

****

The next week was sheer bliss. Lorna had booked a cottage with two bedrooms connected by a comfortable sitting room. Amalie gave herself over to being cosseted and coddled.

Her body was smoothed and soothed with oils and lotions, her feet were treated to a pedicure. Her face was encased in some kind of strange green paste that left it clean and rosy and tingling. Best of all her hair was treated with hot oil then cut much shorter and shaped and trimmed until she hardly recognized the soft pale cap of curls as her own.

Who was this person, she thought, as she looked at her slim, almost boyish figure in the mirror. What would Jonathan have thought? He'd always loved her more generous figure and her longer hair. He loved threading his fingers through her curls.

She cut that line of thought off abruptly. That was then, she reminded herself. This was now. She was going to have to learn to live in the now.

They went shopping. Amalie had always been conservative in her dress and frugal in her shopping. But Lorna would have none of it. She wouldn't allow Amalie even to look at jeans or utilitarian shirts or, for that matter, at price tags.

"This is the tropics, for God's sake. Light weight cottons, gauzy fabrics. Silk, even. And nothing you could ever wear in L.A. Think soft and floating."

"Where would I ever wear soft and floating?" Amalie smiled.

"Buy some and you might find out."

So Amalie bought gauzy pants and tops and soft silks that seemed to float around her as she walked, just to appease Lorna. Then she bought some simple shirts and shorts in her new size, a full two sizes smaller than anything in her closet.

And she slept. And slept. She took naps every afternoon and could barely stay awake through dinner in the resort restaurant in the evenings.

Lorna and Edward didn't seem to mind that she retired early. Edward had decided to remain on St. Luke's with them and had taken a room in the hotel section of the resort. He and Lorna spent their evenings together. Once Amalie was asleep, she and Edward played gin rummy in the sitting room of the cottage and talked into the wee hours.

On the morning of the eighth day Edward flew them back to St. Clement's. Amalie was a changed person. She was still a shadow of her former self, but she was eating once again and sleeping. She smiled occasionally and once she had laughed aloud at some piece of nonsense Edward had said.

****

"Will you be staying on for a while?" Edward asked Lorna once they were back at Amalie's home that evening.

"I won't leave until I know she's out of danger. Besides I have something I want to do here. Something that will hopefully keep

Amalie too busy to allow her time to be depressed. And I'll need your help."

"My help?" The lawyer looked puzzled.

"You remember that surveyor's report you gave Amalie?"

"Of course. The Ansett Plantation property."

"I took it back to L.A. with me and I've had a section of it drawn up into two and three acre lots. I need you to help persuade Amalie that this is something she should consider."

"What, exactly, do you have in mind?"

Lorna told him.

The next afternoon, the two of them presented the plan to Amalie.

She was outraged. "You mean for me to sell off chunks of Ansett Plantation that's been in the family since the seventeen hundreds? How could you?" She was close to tears.

"Just hear us out, Amalie." Lorna took a deep breath and plunged in.

"When you took me out to see that property, you described the plantation house to me so completely, so beautifully, that you made it come alive to me. And having seen it, I wasn't able to get it out of my mind. I want to help you restore it, Amalie, back to the way you described it to me. Right down to the crystal chandeliers and the pianoforte in the drawing room and the bougainvillea climbing up the veranda walls. I want you to restore it to what it once was and turn it into an inn."

Edward chimed in, "This island has no tourist accommodation now. It could use a small, elegant inn."

Amalie looked from one to the other of them. They were serious. She shook her head. "Even if I wanted to do that, and I'm not at all sure I want to, I don't have any money to do it with. It would take a small fortune."

Lorna reasoned with her. "If you sold off just ten or twelve lots on the upper slopes of Mt. Zingara, you'd have enough to get started. I have some savings I'm willing to invest in the project. And once underway we might be able to get a mortgage from the bank to finish the job."

"But Lorna, this isn't a tourist destination. We have mostly black sand beaches and nothing much in the way of shops. Tourists want white sand beaches and they wanted them lined with shops and casinos."

"Don't you understand, Amalie, St.Clement's is that rare find in the Caribbean, an island unspoiled by commercial development. It will appeal to people who would rather hike new trails or go diving in pristine waters than sit in casinos. People who wanted to be some place restful, without the intrusion of thousands of cruise ship passengers clogging streets lined with designer shops. Don't you see what we'd be marketing, Amalie? The Caribbean of people's dreams."

Amalie smiled. "We do have experience in marketing."

Lorna continued. "We can't compete with the Hiltons and Holiday Inns on the larger neighboring islands. That isn't the clientele what we want. We have to focus in the uniqueness of this island, of this inn. There is a market for this sort of retreat. We just had to reach the right travelers."

Edward chimed in. "I think it's a great idea. Would you consider taking me on as a silent partner? I have some spare cash I could invest."

Amalie looked from one to the other. She remembered how beautiful Ansett Plantation House had been. Could they really turn back the clock? Could they make it look like that again?

"I need to sleep on this."

Later that evening, Amalie studied the old lithograph of Ansett Plantation House on the wall of the sitting room. What would Josephina have wanted her to do? Amalie knew the answer. She would have wanted to see the house rebuilt to what it had once been. She wouldn't have cared that some of the land would have to be sacrificed in order to do that. She wouldn't have cared that the house would be used as an inn. She would have thought it a wonderful plan.

The next morning Amalie invited Edward to join them for breakfast and told them of her decision. Lorna was ecstatic. She started making plans immediately.

"I should get back to L.A. soon. We'll mount an advertising campaign for those lots that will knock your socks off. We'll make them so high priced and so exclusive that we'll have people knocking down our doors to be a part of this new development."

Edward asked, "What shall we call it?"

"We have to call it what it is," Amalie said. "Ansett Plantation. Anything else would be unthinkable."

"And the Inn?"

"Ansett House."

"So be it."

Edward spoke up. "There's one thing you haven't considered, Lorna."

"Oh?"

"You'll need government approval to sub-divide the acreage into lots, and government approval to restore the old manor house, especially if you're planning to turn it into an inn. Luckily," he grinned, "one of your partners is a local lawyer with political connections. We'll see how fast we can move things along. Although you must realize that fast is a relative word in the Caribbean."

Two weeks later, Lorna decided that Amalie was sufficiently recovered to be left in Elvirna's care. Especially since Edward had promised to check on her daily.

Amalie, for her part, was a bit relieved to have the beach house once again to herself. She recognized all that Lorna and Edward had done for her in the last month, but she had some things she needed to do. And she needed to do them alone.

She awoke the next morning to Enrico's usual loud announcement of daybreak. She slipped on her bathing suit and went for an early morning swim. She hadn't done that since her return from the past. It was soothing floating on the gentle swells, remembering. She could remember now without tears. Not without pain, but without tears. That was a start.

Today she would do what she must do. What she had been afraid to do while Lorna was with her. She would visit the museum. The portraits would be different, of that she was certain, but how would they differ? Then she would go to the grave yard. There would be changes in the tombstones as well.

These things she had to do to bring some sort of closure. If the portraits were changed, if she saw different dates on his grave, she would have to accept that it was truly over. That she would never see him again. She believed that she was strong enough now to face that.

After breakfast on the veranda, during which Elvirna hovered over her and watched until she had eaten every bite of the omelet and every crumb of the toast, Amalie took the jeep and headed into town. There she parked in the square and walked to the museum.

Gustavia greeted her warmly. "It's so good to see you up and about. I had heard that you weren't well. We were all worried."

269

"Thanks, Gustavia. I'm going to be fine." And at that moment, Amalie realized that it was true. She was going to be all right. "I just wanted to look at the portraits once again."

"Go right on in."

Now that the moment had arrived Amalie felt strangely reluctant. Benstone's portrait would likely still be there, wouldn't it? After all he had been Administrator in eighteen ten. She walked through to the drawing room and looked up. She was so shocked by what she saw that she had to sit down for a moment. She stared at the large picture hanging where Benstone's portrait used to be.

Jonathan was older, perhaps in his forties. His laugh lines were more pronounced. There was even a touch of grey at his temples. He looked...settled. And content. He stood, in the portrait, his arm resting on the shoulder of a boy of perhaps twelve. Clearly his son. Seated to his right was Amalie. A smile played on her lips, as if to say. "I know the secret to happiness." A baby sat on her lap, while a little girl of about eight stood beside her. The girl had Amalie's blond curls and mischievous look. And at Amalie's feet, a little boy – perhaps six years old – sat, cross-legged.

Amalie laughed aloud. "My, Jonathan, you have been busy!" She remembered his threat that he would keep her occupied and out of trouble. It seemed he had done so.

She stood and walked over to the picture to read the caption.

Jonathan Evans, Administrator of St. Clement's, 1824-1840. Shown here with his wife Amalie Ansett Evans and their four children.

"Oh, Jonathan, how wonderful. You were Administrator during the period when the slaves were finally freed. How happy that must have made you."

Amalie sat back down and studied the picture. Somehow it made her feel whole again.

Later, on her way out of the museum, she spoke to Gustavia. "Wasn't there a portrait of an Administrator named Benstone here at one time?"

"Not that I've ever seen. There was briefly Administrator by that name, but I believe he served less than a year. The rumor is that he just disappeared one night. They found later that he had been engaged in some sort of shady dealings, but I don't know any of the particulars."

Amalie was smiling as she left the museum. She walked across the square to the Anglican Church and the old cemetery behind it.

Immediately she spied a pair of graves she had not seen before. Brushing the surface of the old stones she read on one, *Samuel Evans 1784-1848*, and beside it, *Yvette Gerbeaux Evans 1788-1850*. Amalie wondered if his French wife had come from Martinique. She hoped they had been happy.

She moved to Amalie Ansett Evans' grave, close beside Jonathan's. She had lived to be almost seventy. A fine age in that day and time. She would have seen her children grow up and bring her grandchildren to visit her, perhaps even her great-grandchildren.

Amalie sighed with something she recognized as envy.

Finally she moved to Jonathan's grave. She had steeled herself for this but still the tears came. "I did love you well, but not long. Not long enough."

She heard his voice softly singing the next phrase of the tune... "delighting in your company." It was her overactive imagination of course, but she looked up.

He was there. A shadowy figure, not the way she had seen him before. A wavy image, transparent.

"Jonathan!" she cried.

He looked at her with love in his eyes. "I've been granted these few moments with you. This will be our last time together. I must leave and I can't come back. You must live here and I must live there. For me it is easy because I will always have you beside me."

"How can I bear losing you?"

"The blessing and the curse is that you won't remember me. You won't remember any of this."

"I couldn't forget you. Not ever."

"Perhaps someday you will hear an echo from the past. If you believe as I do that..." His voice faded. His image was gone. A melody lingered in the air for a moment and then it, too, was gone.

Amalie sat on her heels beside Jonathan Evans grave, with a sense of loss so great that the pain was beyond endurance.

Gradually she became aware again of her surroundings. What was she doing here in the cemetery? Her cheeks were damp. Why on earth would she have been crying over the grave of a man who died almost two centuries ago?

She had a strange feeling of emptiness, of loss, but why? Shaking her head and drying her eyes, she made her way out of the grave yard and across the square to the jeep.

The workmen were due out at the plantation this morning. They were going to start clearing the weeds and bush out of the foundations. The first steps toward the restoration of Ansett Plantation House were about to begin. She had work to do.

EPILOGUE

Amalie sat back on her heels and surveyed with some satisfaction the stone planter she had just finished building. Perhaps the work wasn't as fine as old Mr. Eustace himself would have done, but he had taught her how to lay the stones so the cement didn't show and to her eye it looked just fine. Tomorrow she would plant bougainvillea in it to match the ones she had planted at the other veranda corners. It would add a nice touch of color and in time it would climb to the second story balcony.

She glanced at her watch. Five o'clock. For a moment she looked out on the calm turquoise sea, at the waves splashing gently on the black sand crescent beach and contemplated taking a quick swim. But no. The guests would be wandering down soon looking for their sunset drinks.

With a small sigh she studied the inn. It had taken eight months longer than they anticipated, but one wing was now up and running. The ten rooms on this side of the complex were finished and most of them were already occupied with guests here for the Christmas holidays. The annex with its ten additional rooms and courtyard swimming pool were well under way and should be finished by spring. Amalie tried to push the cost overruns out of her mind. The money was coming in now. The lots on the hillside had brought in a welcome influx of capitol. They would make it. Just barely, but they would make it.

Amalie smiled. The inn might belong to her but there was no question in her mind as to who was running things. Elvirna's advice had been invaluable. How many times in the last eighteen months had she pulled Amalie's bacon out of the fire? Kept her from getting ripped off by suppliers? Told her what she had to do to keep her workers more or less on schedule?

Then Eleanor Johnston, the woman who'd helped her find Azur Air when she first came to St. Luke's, had been a huge help when it came to getting a government loan. And Edward Sloan. He'd been a rock throughout the whole process. She could never have managed without him to guide her through the tricky waters of dealing with the necessary local government approvals.

She smiled as she remembered yesterday's wedding reception. Two hundred people here at Ansett House and it had gone off without a hitch. Lorna and Edward were delighted with the results. What a handsome couple they made, Lorna in her rose silk and Edward in his formal tropical whites. They should be in Paris by now. The first stop on their honeymoon.

Amalie strolled into the kitchen, poured herself a tall glass of sparkling water and pulled up a chair. "Everything's going well. The guests seem quite happy. And they love your cooking."

Elvirna nodded. "I needs chicken broth for the peanut soup tomorrow night. Six cans. The boat should be in tomorrow. I hope they has the cases we ordered. And the cases of steaks. Mr. Enfield will be passing by in the morning with the lobsters for tomorrow's dinner."

"Sounds great. I'll go uptown for the chicken broth first thing after breakfast. Dunley's should have it."

"Seem to me you should be gettin' cleaned up. You looks like you been playin' in the dirt."

Amalie laughed. "That's exactly what I was doing. I was finishing the last planter for the bougainvillea at the corners of the veranda."

"Well get going. Dinner's at eight."

"Yes, ma'am." Amalie saluted and went back outside.

Wandering out of the kitchen, Amalie surveyed the terrace. Most of the tables were occupied now. The sunset crowd. Everyone had been served and people seemed to be lingering over their rum punches or gin and tonics, chatting from table to table as they watched the sun settle slowly into the sea. Elvirna's son, Johnny, who did double duty as waiter and bartender, was refilling glasses, offering bowls of nuts and chips.

Amalie moved from table to table, chatting, making sure all the guests were satisfied with their accommodation and enjoying their stay. She offered to arrange a dive the next day for one party and a guided hike into the extinct volcano for another. Most guests seemed to be satisfied with the promise of a day of quiet reading on the terrace, or swimming and sunning on the beach.

The guests gradually disappeared back to their rooms to shower and dress for dinner. She should do the same, but she loved this time of day, when no one was around. She walked across the lawn to the cliff. She had placed a small gazebo there and planted jasmine around it. She didn't know what possessed her to go to the expense of the gazebo, but it just seemed right in this spot.

She sat on the bench and looked back at the house with a feeling of pride. It had taken them two years. Two years of hard work on everyone's part. Amalie herself had researched every detail, right down to the proper kind of hardware to use on the shutters and doorknobs. She loved the way it looked. All old stone and yellow brick and clapboard with wide balconies and generous verandas. The center door was open and light spilled out to the veranda and lawn from the huge crystal chandelier just inside the entrance. Amalie knew it was also shedding light on the parquet flooring she had insisted on installing. She had even been able to find a rebuilt antique piano for the drawing room.

It looked now as it had looked two hundred years ago when…

277

Her mind always came to an abrupt halt at that point. She frowned…When what?

"I read that it used to be an important sugar plantation during the years of the slave trade. Is that correct?"

The deep resonant male voice was strangely familiar.

With something akin to shock, Amalie turned toward him and looked up into eyes of a deep, fathomless blue, eyes that she was certain she had seen before. She studied the man. Tall. Sandy colored hair worn a bit longer than was currently fashionable. Wide shoulders, trim waist, and a certain animal grace. He seemed so familiar. Amalie wracked her brain for a name. It was on the tip of her tongue. "You are….?"

He didn't answer for a moment. He seemed as stunned by the encounter as she. He simply stood, glued to the spot, staring at her.

"I'm sorry," he stammered. "It's just…have we met before?"

"I…I don't know. I don't think so."

"Look," his voice seemed a bit shaky. "I know we haven't been formally introduced, but would you have dinner with me tonight? I hear the dining room here is pretty good."

Amalie burst out laughing. "I'm very glad to hear that. I'm the owner." Brushing her hands clean on her shorts, she extended her hand. "Amalie Ansett."

He took her hand it and held it. "I seem to have made an ass of myself, as usual. I apologize. But I ask again, will you have dinner with me?"

"I should be delighted to, Mr…"

"Evans. John Evans. I'm a marine biologist, here from England to set up a research station." His eyes never left her face as he spoke. The words, the ordinary words, were not what his eyes said.

Amalie took a deep breath and tried to break the spell. "Welcome to St. Clement's, Mr. Evans. How long will you be staying?"

"It's John. And I expect to be here for at least five years. Maybe longer if the job materializes the way I hope it will."

"That's good. That's very good."

"And while I'm here I want to try to locate some property that's in our family. According to family lore, when Edward Evans inherited the title and estate back in sixteen forty, the younger Evans brother, James, sought his fortune in the Caribbean, on St. Clement's. I gather there's nothing much left of the place but scrub land and ruins, but we've kept paying the taxes on it and I'd like to see it. Maybe I'll build a house on it. I'll need someplace to live."

"I can help you there. Evans Plantation adjoins this land, Ansett Plantation that belongs to me. We can go see it tomorrow morning if you like."

"That would be wonderful."

"But now, if you'll just give me back my hand, John, I really have to go shower and dress for dinner." Amalie laughed as he looked down at her hand, still clasped in his.

"Oh. Yes, sorry." He released her hand reluctantly.

"The rest of the guests will be coming down, and I must be ready to greet them. But you will sit at my table. We will have dinner together."

Amalie walked toward the inn, her step quicker and her heart lighter than it had been in a very long time. She could feel his eyes following her until she was out of sight.

As she showered Amalie found herself singing,

"And I have loved you well and long,
Delighting in your company."

THE
END